The Memory Monkey

René Ghosh

ISBN 9782953100440

I

Tascha is silent at breakfast and has been for some time now. The radio is on. She's staring off into space when Max walks into the kitchen and looks up at him sharply when he comes into view. She begins to talk as Max bends to kiss her cheek.

"I don't love you anymore."

Her tone indicates she's saying something important, but while she's speaking, Max has no hint as to what it's about, so he just slows his gesture down, his lips reaching her cheek just as she ends her sentence. He stays there, face hovering like a toy run out of batteries, bent over at the waist, his face a breath away from hers. He can smell her shampoo.

"What?"

"I don't love you anymore."

Max sits down, smiles, and waits for her face to smile in return, but it doesn't.

"You know that's not possible," says Max.

"Do I? Do we? We've always been so sure." She shrugs.

He changes the subject, supposes she's pissed off at him for some reason.

"Is there any bread left?" Switching to the cold and factual, he figures, will precipitate whatever reproach she's nurturing toward him. She doesn't get angry.

"There's plenty of bread left," she says. She gets up to make him toast, serves him coffee, adds milk.

"They had a new blend at the market," she mentions. Her voice is perfect domesticity.

Max bites into his toast. "It's just not possible," he says through a full mouth. "I've seen equations and shit."

She shrugs, looks away. "I don't think I even like you

anymore. I don't recognize myself in anything you do."

He takes another bite of toast. The crunch is loud and seems to irritate her, though as he scans the face of the woman he loves, he can find no salient, identifiable proof of irritation.

...

'You know what,' says Max to himself, 'I'm not going to open the shop.' He prints a sign and chooses the words carefully:

'Due to family issues, the shop will remain closed for the next few days. We deeply regret any inconvenience.'

Tascha finds the sign on the front window and frowns. "What the fuck, man," she says, yanking it off.

She calls out to him, "Why don't you take a few days and deal with your family issues?" She pulls out the postcard racks, one rack per hand, arm muscles taut and confident as she drags them backwards toward the front of the shop.

"What did I do?" asks Max. "Tell me what I did."

Tascha wipes her hands on the back of her jeans.

...

On Sunday, to Max's surprise, she gets ready for church. Because she's been drifting out of the relationship, he supposes that she must be chafing at more or less all of her constraints. But no, she actually seems eager to go. For the first time that week, she even speaks to him kindly.

"Are you coming to church?"

"I don't need a bullshit sermon right now."

"It's not bullshit. We just never gave it a chance. Lately, I don't know... I've been listening more closely. There's a lot there that I can connect to. That we can connect to."

She nods in agreement with herself.

...

After the sermon, Max stands outside the church gripping a polystyrene cup of tea, rocking back and forth from his heels to the balls of his feet and squinting up at the sun. Frin comes out to join him, carrying his own tea in a polystyrene cup. A polystyrene cup of slightly larger format.

Frin stands next to him.

"So," says Frin, "I hear Tascha is free?" Like so many other Extrapolists, Frin worries that his sexual experiences will be insufficient to last over in the afterlife until the time of his next rebirth.

Max avoids looking at him. "Tascha's mine. Don't you touch her."

Frin makes a deprecating sound in his throat, as though having trouble swallowing. "That's not how she puts it."

Max scowls at the sun. He doesn't reply. He'd like to chuck his tea into Frin's face, but the tea is already cool and wouldn't inflict any damage.

"That was a good sermon today," remarks Frin.

"I hardly listened to it. I've been preoccupied. I guess you noticed."

"Get over yourself, man."

Frin heads back inside the church. Max watches him go, trying to picture the other man's form the way Tascha might, now that she's free. Frin is a tall, lanky man, with strong shoulders built up through physical conditioning. He has an arrogant face. Max can't imagine what it feels like to be attracted to a man and decides that it's useless to even try. He crumples his polystyrene cup and takes it inside to throw away.

He approaches Tascha in the reception hall where all the churchgoers are massed following the sermon. Tascha is speaking with a friend of hers, a thirtysomething woman.

"Are you ready to go?" asks Max.

"I'm going to stay," replies Tascha with an apologetic smile. Max guesses that the smile is only apologetic for her friend's benefit.

Max would like to add something, but she turns back to her friend to resume the conversation.

...

Max goes over inventory in the storage room of the shop. For every item type, he checks the amount on a set of printed-out pages, then counts them with his right hand. He touches every item to make sure it exists when you touch it as well as when you look at it. He murmurs each item type aloud, like he's doing a roll call.

"Hiking boot chains, speckled steel. Water flask, bacteria-free spout."

He doesn't notice Baran entering the storage room. Baran stands right behind him, waiting for him to finish the row he's on.

"Well, at least you're working," says Baran when Max reaches the end of the row.

Max turns around. "Hey Baran. What do you mean?"

"You know. What with Tascha leaving you."

Max shakes his head. He turns back to the inventory, starting a new row. "Tascha hasn't left me. It's just time for us to discover new people."

Baran looks down a moment. Takes a deep breath.

"That sounds like Extrapolist bullshit. Yeah, she wants to discover other people. That's just typical after being married for so long. You know, it's not that I don't feel any sympathy for you, but this goes beyond Tascha wanting to get it on with other men. I mean, good for her, right? But come, let's sit down and talk."

Max sighs. Baran is married to Sinvia. Another Institute couple.

Pretending to be making progress in his inventory, Max asks "Tell me, has Sinvia been with other men?"

"I don't know. I don't ask her. I don't care. This isn't what this is about, you know that."

"Well I still love Tascha, so I don't have any insight for you."

"Come on, let's get some coffee, talk about this? I'll work the machine. I know how, you know. I sometimes sneak into the shop when it's closed and make myself a cup."

"Please give me back the store keys."

They head to the front of the shop. There are three long tables there, set in front of a bar behind which sits a coffee machine, too gleamingly luxurious for an outdoor equipment shop. It's an admission that most of the clients of the outdoors shop are used to a certain level of comfort that follows them around where they go, even when they're traveling to get close to nature.

Max plops into a chair. Baran goes behind the bar and busies himself with the coffee machine.

"What am I going to do?" says Max. "How am I supposed to live without Tascha? She's a hard woman, but you can lean on her, you know? I can't picture myself with anyone else. I'm going to be lonely."

"Bullshit." Baran's voice sails over to him from across the bar like a projectile. "Other people do it all the time. We've seen them do it right under our noses. They meet someone, have sex a few times, and then these chemicals get going in their heads and suddenly, their loyalties realign themselves. It's organic. Tascha is out there right now doing it even as we speak. We're human, just like everyone else."

"OK, that's painful, the image of Tascha with some other guy. Let's just avoid —"

"The other guy is almost certainly Frin, by the way. I was watching them this morning at church after you left. I didn't need to hear what they were saying, their body language was so obvious."

"I don't want to imagine that. It's a stab."

Baran chuckles. "You know, I don't think Frin's the kind of guy to let her be on top. How do I know that? I don't even know how I know that."

Max crosses his arms on the table and lays his head over them. Baran has prepared the two coffees and carries them around the bar. He sits facing Max.

"There's a coffee next to your left elbow," he says, putting the cup down. "If you move too brusquely, you'll spill it all over the floor."

Baran slurps some coffee. "If it happened to Tascha, it could happen to any of the other Institute couples. It could happen to Sinvia and me, to the others."

Max mumbles through his arms, "I don't care about the others. I don't care about you."

"No, you just care that Tascha is getting smothered under Frin's sweaty skin right now."

"Shut the fuck up."

"She's squealing in a high-pitched tone that she never once used with you and that you wouldn't even recognize."

"Shut. Up"

"She's trembling in his arms, feeling an electrical surge soar through her muscles, shocked by what Frin has revealed to her about her own body."

"Would you just stop?"

Baran chuckles again, then becomes pensive. "Max, my friend, the reason I've come to you today is not to assuage your troubles, which are, of course, your own. It's just that, in my opinion, Tascha freeing herself from the couples conditioning is an opportunity. I understand that you don't see it that way right now, in your advanced state of self-pity."

"You want to sleep with Tascha too."

"No. Well, no. Whatever. If Tascha has broken conditioning, that means she may be able to access her pre-conditioning memories."

Max meets Baran's stare straight on, expecting his friend to be cowed by it, but Baran leisurely slurps more coffee and pursues, "You know, Sinvia has really let herself go these past years. She does no sports, neglects her grooming, takes no interest in conversation. Most other men in my situation would be looking to switch partners, but the thought doesn't occur to me, at least not on any emotional level. I'm still deeply attached to her. I can't even imagine my world without her, the same way you can't imagine yours without Tascha."

"Because we will never replace these women," says Max.

Baran shrugs. "She can sure as fuck imagine her world without you, though. But don't worry, Max. I have this intuition that maybe your world won't fall apart at all. How do I know that? I don't know how I know that. But, what's going to happen is, you'll suffer a little and then just move on, maybe even reinvent a new life for yourself. And if that happens, well, maybe we don't need to be protected from the pre-conditioning memories anymore. We could go back to the institute and tell Doctor Tescar that we're healed and ask him to give us back all our old memories. Wouldn't that be great?"

Max grimaces. "Those memories were horrible enough that no one would ever want them back. And even if we did, there's no technology that can give you back your memories. It's not like a digital recording that you can just pop into and out of your head."

Baran stands. "I think the memories are all still in our heads. I don't know about you, but I'm tired of living with this large segment of my life missing. Other people talk about their childhood memories with so much pleasure. That could be us, Max. Not all our old memories are bad. There has to be some salvageable ones in the bunch that'll enrich our sense of ourselves. We should unlock those."

Baran carries his empty coffee cup back to the bar and leaves it there to stain the counter. He says, "I'm going back to my shabby wife, the one I've been conditioned to love forever," heading for the exit. "Thank you for coffee."

Max calls out, "I'm not conditioned to love you and I don't think that I —"

...

Tascha comes home at four in the morning. Max is sitting in the kitchen with a cold cup of tea. She walks past him in the dark and cries out when he brushes her sleeve.

"Oh! What are you doing up?"

"I was waiting for you."

"Great. Now we're both going to be tired tomorrow at the shop."

She's moving out of the kitchen as she says it, moving toward the hallway and the stairs that lead to the bedroom.

As she reaches the kitchen door, Max says, "You smell like another man."

Tascha shoots back "You can't smell me from over there," but she hesitates at the door anyway.

"Well, I imagine that you smell like another man."

"Let's not make a big deal out of this, OK? We're all just large groups of molecules hurtling through space and the universe, yielding to forces that are beyond our comprehension. We exist for a short time and then we don't. We should let those forces allow us to express our beauty and our meaning."

Max nods. He gazes over at his wife, appreciating that, even though she doesn't love him anymore, she still retains enough respect to stay there listening. Taking his thoughts into consideration.

"Baran came by today. Said he saw you with Frin."

Tascha laughs and shakes her head. "Small towns. It's great until suddenly it's not. So, is everyone talking?"

"Well Baran is talking because he and Sinvia are an Institute couple, obviously. Are your memories coming back, Tascha? Is that it?"

Tascha looks away. She taps the door frame twice with her palm, as though suddenly worried that the house is not solid. "Nothing is coming back. But I wish it would. I'd really love to know who I was before I became just half of whatever you and I are."

"Whatever you and I are, Tascha, I refuse to believe that it's nothing. Or that it's made up. Or that it's fake."

Tascha shrugs. "It's late, we have to open the shop in the morning. Are you coming to bed?"

"Do you want me to?"

"No, but half of that bed belongs to you. I don't want to be mean about it."

"I'll sleep on the couch."

Tascha nods and pushes off the door frame, moving resolutely toward the stairs. Her footsteps are heavier than usual. She's drunk. Max sips his cold tea, feeling the bitterness roll over his tongue. Mentally, he replays her sentence about molecules hurtling through space and wonders where that came from. It could have been a book, but Tascha never reads anything and isn't drawn to science. He supposes that she's quoting someone else's affirmation to her. The kind of affirmation you offer to make someone else feel good about feeling free. The kind of affirmation you offer someone to draw them out of their shell.

Upstairs in the bedroom he hears Tascha bumping into a

piece of furniture. He hears her cry out, "Fuck! Fucking shit!"

2

A few weeks later, Tascha walks into the shop. She's acting like a client, scrunching her nose at a few products, taking a box down from the top shelf to peer at it closely before putting it back. She sighs and comes up to the counter behind which Max stands stone-faced.

"Hey," she says. Her face is blank.

"Is there something I can help you with?" replies Max in a drone-like voice.

"You haven't been coming to church."

"You came to the shop to ask me that? You could just come downstairs anytime and just ask me."

"I thought it'd be best if we each had our space."

"We live in the same house! This is ridiculous. So, is our staircase the no-man's land?"

Tascha clears her throat and taps with both hands on the counter, as though they've just reached the drum solo portion of the conversation. She taps, then stops. Then she taps some more.

"How've you been, Max?"

Max shrugs. "I'm OK. Though, I really wish you'd have told me that you intended to stop working in the shop because it gets a little hectic sometimes."

Tascha snorts. "No it doesn't. Hardly anyone ever comes in. If there were any competition in this town we'd be out of business."

"'We'. Well, if ever it does get hectic, I'll be quickly submerged. Sometimes I'm ringing up a purchase and someone is waiting over there for a coffee, and they give me this dirty look even though they can tell I'm busy."

Tascha chuckles.

"Seriously, they look at me like I should just drop the

ongoing purchase and go make their coffee."

"Well, you sound OK."

"I'm OK. Well... You know me, I'm good at giving things up. I never thought I'd have to give you up, though. This is like the ultimate test. I'm passing, I guess."

"Oh." Tascha, oddly touched, pulls her head back and looks at him in surprise. "I'm glad then."

"Do you care?"

"What?"

"Do you care how I am?"

"Of course I care." She looks back down at the counter and taps it some more. "You haven't been coming to church though."

Max sighs. "Why would I bother going there anymore? The only reason we went there in the first place was to register our presence in the community. But there's no 'us' anymore so we don't need the community. Also, I've been told you're using the church as a dating field."

Tascha shrugs. "Maybe a little. I'm just testing my new freedom. The men don't mean anything to me."

"Why do you want me to come to church anyway? To admire how you navigate between these meaningless men?"

"No. It doesn't feel right that you're not there with me. You're my soul mate. That doesn't change just because our physical bodies are separating."

"Oh, fuck off with the soul mate shit."

"It's true, Max! We've been together for so many years, now. That's not coincidence. We're intertwined, you and I. Living together, being together, it had meaning. It doesn't just disappear."

"Doesn't it, though? You know I'm good at giving things up. So now, watch me give up intertwinedness. Watch me throw it out like the garbage that it is."

Tascha sighs. She says, "OK." She taps the counter a few more times, as though the conversation song has just ended with a drum aftershock. Then, she turns and walks toward the shop entrance.

Max watches her retreating form and notes what a

beautiful sight it is, a woman walking away from you. It states that, wherever you happen to be, there's some other point in space that's probably even better. He watches her go and mentally gives her a thirty percent chance of turning around before disappearing from view, if only because she came to see him. But she doesn't, so maybe she didn't, really.

...

Grudgingly, not fully recognizing his own reasons for doing so, he goes to church that Sunday, stepping through the narrow door of the Extrapolist church building, last of all the churchgoers. The door opening is purposefully narrow so that people can only enter the building one at a time. People with larger frames sometimes have trouble squeezing through. In certain cases allowances are made for the very large ones to enter through the side door, provided people never enter two at once. The symbolism holds that the physical church is a metaphor for the physical universe and that souls are perfectly alone until they enter into it. Within the church there are both individual and group seats. Custom holds that no one should get accustomed to any seat but rather change seating every week.

On the far wall, behind the preaching stage, a different Community Thought is printed every week in large letters. Max gazes at this week's Community Thought as he sits down.

The sentence looms, 'We are all groupings of molecules. We hurtle through space and the universe. We are subject to forces beyond our comprehension.'

Max strikes his forehead, exclaiming "So that's where she got it!". He turns to his right to explain himself and finds he's sitting beside Frin.

Frin nods to him with a pinched smile.

"Tascha said that to me this week," explains Max, pointing to the Community Thought. "I thought it sounded stupid, to tell you the truth. It seems so much deeper when it's written in big letters like that."

Frin nods. "Well, it's not wrong, anyhow."

"You're a real smug bastard, you know that?" says Max. "You always have to say something to look smart."

Frin puts a hand on his shoulder. "We're inside the church here. Let's be together, Max."

Max, without looking at the hand resting on his shoulder yet acutely aware of it, says "I'll be together with you just as soon as you admit that you're a smug bastard."

Frin lets his hand slip off of Max's shoulder. "I am together with you, Max, even if you aren't together with me."

"You're together with me through fucking my wife, you smug bastard. Did you come here with Tascha today?"

"No, I didn't come here with Tascha today." Frin sighs. "I thought you did."

Max swivels in his seat and looks around for Tascha. He spots her to the far right, sitting in a single seat. She meets his gaze and briefly waves at him.

...

The Guide reads a passage from the Book of Past Lives, about standing waves on a lake and the way they rebound and traverse one another. Max thinks it would have been a prettier passage if it had just remained as an evocative description of waves and let the audience extrapolate the spiritual ramifications, but it veers into a tedious explanation, cutting away all mystery, so he sighs loudly. Frin chuckles. Max tries to hate him but can't refrain a wave of pleasure at making someone chuckle.

...

After the service there's a reception in the church basement. Sandwiches are served at one table, pies at another, and the last table holds the drinks. Tascha stands in the sandwiches line and waves Max over when he enters the basement.

"Go stand in the pie line," she orders. "Get me a slice of pie. I'll stand in the sandwich line and get you a sandwich."

Max gives her a weary look. "Do you really need a sandwich and a slice of pie?"

"I won't know until I've tried both. Hurry! People are still coming in, the lines are filling quickly."

Max stands in the pie line and shuffles forward. Tascha stands in the sandwich line, shifting nervously from foot to foot, tilting her head sideways and gauging the amount of sandwiches of each kind that are left on the table. There's never enough food for everyone at these receptions.

Max gets a slice of pie and waits in a corner for her to join him. She walks up to him bearing two sandwiches and fiercely whispers, "Why didn't you get two slices of pie? Didn't you tell them it was for both of us?"

"It wasn't really for both of us. We were both in a line, so each getting the equivalent of a single portion of food. By combining our single portions we get a couple's portion. Though... I see you weren't thinking like that."

Tascha pushes a sandwich toward his face. "Here."

"I don't want it. I'm not hungry."

"Just take it."

"I don't want it."

"I need to free a hand up to take the slice of pie."

"I'll hold it for you."

"Just take the sandwich."

"I don't want the sandwich."

"Trade the sandwich for the pie. Come on! I want to get a drink before there's nothing left."

"No."

Tasha squeezes the sandwich in her right hand, compressing it beyond recognition into a tight roll of concentrated calories, then reaches out with the same hand and grabs the slice of pie from him, her crooked fingers stabbing at his hand. Max stands there motionless, afraid that any action on his part will result in food falling to the floor. She expects him to struggle though, and when he doesn't her stabbing becomes more erratic.

Max says, "Don't pry! I'll give it to you. Stop stabbing at me, just calm down."

Tascha stuffs the whole compressed sandwich from her right hand into her mouth, then reaches out and grabs the slice of pie from him. She mumbles, "Thank you!", fiercely sarcastic through a full mouth, and storms off toward the drinks table.

He watches her in the drinks lineup, shifting nervously, swaying to the side to check up on the progress ahead.

Frin comes to stand with him. "Can I speak with you?"

"Fuck off, Frin. I know you slept with Tascha even though I specifically told you not to."

Frin shrugs. "Well, that's what I came to talk to you about. I'd like to apologize."

"Fuck you and fuck your apologies too." He keeps his eye on Tascha in the drinks lineup. She's almost at the table and has only two more people in front of her. He hears Frin's voice, watches Tascha, and can't help but imagine them together having sex.

Frin says, "I'll be leaving town soon. I'll also be leaving the Extrapolist church for a while. I realized, after sleeping with Tascha, that I hadn't really wanted to, that I'd just been swept along by the group-think. Groups are a wonderful thing, but then you let them think for you and only the loudest, most provocative ideas really circulate. It makes you lazy. It makes you forget what you really want."

"Will you fuck off?"

"I hear your anger."

"I don't care what you hear. I'm glad you're leaving town. You can go to hell."

Erek, the Extrapolist Guide, has been approaching. He overhears Max's last remark.

"Whoa guys, what's going on here? This is the Extrapolist church, there's no such thing as hell in Extrapolism."

"Well," says Max, "there should be. It'd keep us all walking a morally narrower road. This fucker here," he gestures toward Frin as though throwing a ball, "slept with Tascha. There should be some kind of hell for fuckers like him."

"Our destinies are linked to people in ways that can only be understood by exploring those bonds," says Guide Erek.

"You see?" Says Frin. "That's exactly the kind of group-think shit that landed me in this situation. What I did wasn't cool, man! I ended this guy's relationship!"

"Well," says Guide Erek, "I don't know enough about the situation, but I can tell you this: things are not defined by the ways in which they end. They continue through the way each intended."

Max scoffs. "That's really appreciated, Guide. Really puts a bandage on things. Like, one of those bandages that are too small for the wound and end up sticking adhesive in the wound part and prevent it healing properly because it rips the scab when you need to pull it off."

Frin guffaws. "Like, seriously!"

"Laughter is good, and soothing," says Guide Erek. "Just: remember what I said anyways, OK?"

"I'm done with Extrapolism," says Frin.

"I will miss you," says Erek with a note of finality.

"I won't," says Max. "As far as I'm concerned, he can drive off a cliff."

"We are all connected to one another," says Guide Erek. "A part of you would drive off that cliff with him."

"We are so much more interconnected than I'd like," says Max.

Frin says nothing but nods, hands in his pockets. He's a difficult man to hate, standing as he is, looking detached. His face remains arrogant, but it looks regretfully so, like he never chose to look arrogant and can do nothing about it.

Tascha has gotten her drink and is trying to keep the cup upright as she bites from her sandwich. She finished the slice of pie while waiting in line.

...

Frin packs a few suitcases toward the end of the week. He tells his friends and fellow churchgoers that he's leaving the city and doesn't yet know where he'll go, planning to live on his savings until he finds a place where he wants to stay. His friends are puzzled at the sudden need to leave. "Why?" they ask him. "Why now? What's changed?"

He hasn't been the same since spending the night with Tascha.

Guide Erek comes to see him at home one evening,

unannounced.

"May I come in?" asks Erek.

Frin hesitates. "Come in," he says finally, "but you won't change my mind about leaving."

"I don't intend to," replies Guide Erek, with maybe a little too much enthusiasm.

Frin's eyes are circled in grey. He hasn't been sleeping well. He's been awaking exhausted to find his sheets crumpled and drenched with sweat, his mind racing with the aftershock of images that he can't recall, but nevertheless he still feels their violence. He's sure that, every night as he tries to sleep, something takes hold of his mind and snatches it right from his consciousness like taking a rug out from under someone's feet. He suspects it came from Tascha but he can't explain how he knows this, beyond the obvious reason that it started the day after they spent their first night together.

Guide Erek sits across from him in his living room, leaning forward at the waist, hands pressed together and resting on his knees. The image of selfless, serene listening.

"Can I offer you a beer?" asks Frin.

"Sure," says Erek.

"All I have is citrus-flavored, light beer, though. Is that alright?"

Erek shrugs, his earnest gaze never wavering away from Frin. "Whatever you have will be nice, Frin."

"A lot of people don't like beer with added flavor. They feel as though the traditional purity of the drink is being soiled."

"Frin, I know you're leaving and it's not my place at all to convince you to stay. We all have our different paths to follow and that's totally alright. It wouldn't be right if I didn't attempt to listen to your reasons for leaving though, and if I can, try to help you find clarity within them."

Frin nods. "Tascha is possessed by something," he says. "I think she gave it to me. It's some kind of mental parasite. I just want to get away from here. I feel as though I were being punished. I feel really bad toward Max."

Erek nods.

"None of this is compatible with the Extrapolist views, I know," adds Frin. "I know the church views all interactions as enriching and some more than others. I'm just convinced that I've added some kind of destructive weave to the one I picked up from Tascha."

Erek frowns slightly, makes as if to speak.

"Her soul is diseased," adds Frin. "I don't know how Max has survived all these years with her. Maybe he's immune. I don't know."

Erek breathes deeply. "I'll take that beer if the offer still holds."

3

The smokers at Empiricole take their breaks in the parking lot. The building is a large rectangular structure, padded in a reflective aluminum that makes their breaks sweaty in the summer months.

Rialdy walks out of the building, one hand in his pocket, the other one carrying a folder with notes for his upcoming meeting. Sheila is standing outside, smoking. Her hair is up in a bun. She has excellent posture and a graceful arch in her lower back where her blouse tucks into her work skirt.

"Hey Sheila."

She arches her eyebrows and flicks out her chin. "Hey."

Rialdy scans the parking lot. "Have you seen a limo pull up? The Aranacian group is coming. These guys only travel by limo. It's all about prestige. But, they rent the limos, so it's like they're a bunch of kids going to their prom, rather than gangsters."

Sheila doesn't laugh. She shakes her head. "No limos on the horizon. I'll keep you updated." She glances up at him, studying his face, blowing out smoke.

Rialdy hones in on her cigarette. She's holding it in one hand, the other hand holding her wrist.

"Can I get one of those off you?" he asks, pointing to it.

She nods and pulls out her pack. She waits for him to light up.

"You know," she says, "I was mad at you for a while. I was so mad I could have slapped you, hard."

Rialdy nods, handing her back her lighter. "I guess I didn't behave toward you the way I should have."

"You just disappeared. You know, I hadn't asked for anything from you." She waves it off. "But, whatever. How're things? How're you?" She drags on her cigarette, looking away, as though she's forgotten he's even there.

"I'm good. Anna and I are trying to conceive a baby together."

Sheila chuckles. "Really? You? You're going to be a father?"

"Yeah. How is that funny?"

"You'll make a terrible father. You'll be one of those jackasses at the playground who wear sunglasses and stare at their phone all the time, organizing their evening for when the kids'll be in bed and they can head out for some real fun."

"Well. I won't be that guy."

"Good luck, in any event." Sheila's voice is placating. She seems to regret the barb.

From the street just beyond the parking lot, a limo slows, then veers into it. Rialdy hastily puts out his cigarette on the dirty ashtray/garbage tin that sits on top of a black metal post next to the door. It has a little incline that allows for the cigarette to be extinguished, then let go of, to roll down through a slot into the underlying container. Rialdy's cigarette somehow misses it and spills onto the ground in a cascade of ash and red cinders.

"We're in business. These guys have money to spend on our shit. Wish me luck."

"Good luck, Rialdy. I'm sure they'll be impressed."

Rialdy hesitates, thinking of something nice to say. "Thanks for the cigarette." He nods at her, then heads back into the building.

...

The Aranacian group is composed of three men, all portly, all in suits that look expensive but also look like the imitation of even more expensive suits. Their handshakes are bone-crushing but curt, as though they've been working out for something exciting and strenuous and are eager to get back to it after this meeting ends.

Miles, the head of sales at Empiricole, is conducting the meeting. He has a thinning canopy of hair that flutters upward and buttresses his expression of being saddled with worry. His laptop screen reflects off his steel-rimmed glasses as he moves through slides listing Empiricole's prestigious clients and showing figures of growth in in-app code encryption.

Miles drinks tea. Whatever recipient he uses to drink it in, he holds it cupped in both hands as though to warm them from the beverage. He believes that his particular tea of choice holds deep health benefits and this is how he signifies, even when no one is around, that he's receiving wholesome goodness from it. He doesn't add sugar because it doesn't require any. Also, he's persuaded himself that he doesn't like sugar even though he does. Miles has sat in at numerous Japanese tea ceremonies. He's proud to say that he can sit at these ceremonies for hours and never budge a muscle.

Rialdy stands for a good portion of the presentation, close to the screen where the slides are being projected, gazing up at it frequently. After Miles' introduction, it's his turn to talk.

"In-app encryption is the only way to properly ensure that your code will never be violated," he says.

He pauses deliberately. "I like to ask a question at the beginning of these presentations, which is: why have we never been decimated by giant insects? Does anyone know the answer to that?"

He looks in turn at each of the three Aranacians seated there. He realizes he can't remember any of their names. He generally makes a point of listening intently when someone speaks their name, focusing on the face and creating a mental snapshot with the name included as a caption, but today he forgot to and can't address them individually.

He answers his own question.

"It's because insects don't have endoskeletons, they have exoskeletons, basically shells on the outside of their bodies. It serves its purpose for small bodies, but any insect that was human sized would be incapable of supporting its own weight, whereas we can because we carry our skeleton on the inside." He pauses, letting it sink in. Two of the

Aranacians stare at him blankly, the third one is texting on his phone.

"Code security is the same way," he pursues. "If you want to ensure your code isn't violable, you have to protect it at the code level, from the inside. Empiricole Crypter is the premier solution for achieving this, with a completely integrated solution, from login to storage."

The texting Aranacian looks up. "What does this mean, 'integrated'?"

Rialdy repeats the word in Aranacian. Three sets of eyebrows shoot up.

"You speak Aranacian!" one of them exclaims. He laughs and looks at the other two. One of them laughs too, then throws his empty polystyrene coffee cup at him.

Miles and Rialdy exchange a look. Miles' look is saying, 'These men are large children. Adapt your presentation to just such an audience.'

"We like to maintain a body of experts who are keenly sensitive to the international market," says Miles to the Aranacians. They ignore him. The one who just spoke says to Rialdy, "Your boss likes to spend his weekends cleaning between his toes." The Aranacians guffaw. Rialdy laughs nervously, looking furtively at Miles, then away.

He finishes the presentation. The Aranacians ask no questions.

"Moving forward," says Miles, "we should schedule a demo with your own code."

The Aranacians stand up.

"We are in Montreal for the evening," they say to Miles. "Can your boy Rialdy show us some fun?"

"Oh, I believe he can," offers Miles generously. "Rialdy, I'm sure you know some good places to take these gentlemen for a good meal and a cocktail?"

Rialdy spends a moment with his mouth open. Then, "Of course. I know some places."

"Don't bring the boss," says the Aranacian who's apparently the funny one, again in Aranacian. "The boss is not a fun guy."

...

Rialdy phones his girlfriend.

"Tace? I'll be home late. I have to show some clients a good time. I know tonight is conception night, but we can still do it when I get home. If you're sleeping I'll just wake you up. I won't conceive with you in your sleep, don't worry."

"No," says Tace, "don't wake me up. And don't call it conception. We're making a baby." Rialdy winces at the word 'baby'. He's grateful she can't see his face.

"I'll wake you up. We can maintain the schedule."

"No, If I'm sleeping it's because I need to sleep. So, don't wake me up."

"OK. But just, I was totally prepared to wake you up."

He returns to his office he shares with four other coworkers. The Aranacians are waiting for him there. One of them is sitting at his desk, going through his personal belongings in the drawers of the small wheeled cabinet that sits beside his workstation. The other two are leaning against his desk.

"I'll meet you downtown in a few hours, if you like," said Rialdy. He stares at the Aranacian going through his belongings, thinking it'll shame him, but the Aranacian continues to rummage.

"Can I help you with something?" asks Rialdy.

"You people are supposed to be security experts, but you don't even lock your personal cabinets."

"There's nothing of professional interest in there."

The Aranacian slams the drawer shut. "Let's go now."

Rialdy said, "How about I join you downtown? I still have some work to finish up here."

"This is your work. Let's go. Fun time starts now." The seated Aranacian licks his lips and rubs his hands together.

Rialdy thinks, 'What does he think is going to happen? How much fun does he think we're going to have, a bunch of men who don't know each other, having dinner?"

"I just have to talk to Miles for a second," he says, and leaves his office space headed toward Miles'.

Miles is sitting at his desk playing with a multi-jointed plasticized cardboard toy that has the company name and Empiricole logo printed on it. The logo becomes entirely visible only when the puzzle is reconstituted. He hands it to Rialdy when he walks in. "I forgot to give this to the Aranacians."

"Miles, this is embarrassing. They want to go out like, right now."

"So? It beats doing actual work."

"I can't remember their names."

"Ah. Names are important. You should always make the effort to remember people's names."

"Remind me what they are?"

Miles gazes up at the ceiling a moment, silently mouthing words that Rialdy suspects aren't real words but rather a pantomime to highlight his name-recalling abilities.

"The one with the hair brushed back that looks like it shouldn't hold in that flat a position, like a wheat field that's been blown by wind and should have ripped but remains strangely intact save a permanent bend, of a kind of monotonous brown color, with jowly cheeks, is Azgeviu. He's a project manager, the more operational of the three."

"Azgeviu, got it." Azgeviu was the funny one, the one who'd been rummaging through his personal belongings.

"Then, there's the largest one, with a belly that juts out at sternum level, a sure sign that he uses human growth hormone, probably trains in some violent martial art. His face is large and squarish, with a buzz cut indicating contained fury. That's Teoko. He's the proxy client from the business side of their company."

"I don't think I agree with you about the contained fury. Some people just get buzz cuts from early childhood on and never feel the need to change. He's probably just conservative."

"The third one —"

"— no need for that, I'll identify him by elimination —"

"— Is the short one, the one who wears a serious face but you can tell he's rather detached and possibly inwardly aching to start a new life in some artistic field. His hair is longer. I get the impression he recently cut off a ponytail. Anyway, that's Frimiu, and he's in charge of purchases, which worries me because, well, he's detached. I could see him denying the purchase because he can't feel the need for our product. He's the guy you need to convince tonight."

"OK Miles."

"Have a good evening."

"Oh hey, Miles? How would you describe me if someone didn't remember my name and you needed to describe me to him or her?"

Miles takes a moment to consider, appreciating the question. He picks up a cup with some tea left in the bottom and gives it a swirl. "Hmm", he says. Then, he looks up. "Skinny nervous-looking guy. Tries to look cool but looks needy."

"Fuck you, Miles."

"Have a good evening with those crazies. Make them want code-level encryption."

...

The Aranacians are blasting a form of rap/heavy metal in the limo on the way downtown. From the way they bob their heads forward and tap their burly fingers against car seats and the window bases, they look more youthful than they did earlier at the meeting. Rialdy gives them an address which they read to the chauffeur, who replies in Aranacian. Apparently, they rented the limo from an Aranacian business.

"How is it that you have an Aranacian name and speak Aranacian, Rialdy?" asks Teoko. He asks the question with provocation, as though an Aranacian name were something that should be earned.

"My mother was from Aranacia," replies Rialdy. His pronunciation of Aranacian is second-generation immigrant and they pick up on it.

"Why did your mother come to live in Canada?"

"She came here as an exchange student. Met my father, stayed."

Teoko nods and goes back to tapping his fingers and bobbing his head. A guitar solo comes on and all three Aranacians air-guitar with painful grimaces and eyes clenched shut.

They get off downtown. Teoko tells the chauffeur they won't be needing his services for the evening and sends him off.

"Let's eat!"

Rialdy looks at his watch. "It's only 6 o'clock."

"Take us where they have the biggest hamburgers imaginable!"

They eat at Moto Central. The hamburgers are so high that they are served pierced through with long, dangerous-looking toothpicks from top bun to bottom bun, through multiple meat patties and tomato slices. The Aranacians eat with their hands and wipe their greasy fingers on napkins that they seem to be sharing from a large pile on the table, picking them up at random, crumpling them and throwing them back before diving back into their burgers and fries.

Rialdy tries to steer the conversation toward code security. He asks about their business and receives only vague answers. Teoko answers any business-oriented question.

"It's not because our code is especially precious, but we'd like to have it developed in cheaper places, so we have to provide our core components to them without letting them in on any industrial secrets. Much of our code base was built by the military before being provided to private companies."

Rialdy tries to find a followup question and can't think of one. He feels useless here, trying to drum up business for Empiricole and having no idea how to go about it. Speaking Aranacian doesn't come easily to him. He struggles to find words, even common ones, and feels constrained by syntax and word construction. He imagines his dead mother listening to him speak, feels guilty and awkward, wishes he'd learned to speak her language better.

After dinner, the Aranacians want to go to a club. Rialdy

takes them to the Café d'Eté, where twentysomethings gyrate to distortion-heavy post-something music with heavily saturated voice tracks. It's the closest thing he can find to heavy metal. The clubs that played heavy metal all disappeared a decade ago.

The four men stand by the rail overlooking the dance floor, on the first floor, sipping drinks. After some time watching, Frimiu descends onto the dance floor and begins to dance. He holds his fists up near his ears, turning around slowly, sensuously, eyes shut. Rialdy, Azgeviu and Teoko watch him from the rail. Azgeviu and Teoko laugh as Frimiu gets too close to a girl, opens his eyes, tries to throw his arms around her and gets shoved by the girl's boyfriend.

"The little man is going to fight!" exclaims Azgeviu. "You will see how Aranacians are good wrestlers." Apparently, Rialdy is no longer a bona fide Aranacian to them.

"I should go home now," says Rialdy, peering at his watch.

"Wait," says Teoko. He points to Frimiu on the dance floor who's shoved back against the girl's boyfriend and has started to take off his jacket. He has it halfway down his arms when the other man swings and catches him on the nose with a punch.

Teoko and Azgeviu erupt in laughter. Downstairs, two large and muscular bouncers converge on the belligerents from opposite ends of the dance floor. Frimiu, bleeding from his nose, has time to rush his opponent, pick him up over his shoulder, stand, make half a turn, and slam the man to the floor before the bouncers reach them, yanking Frimiu up and off the prone man, who doesn't move as Frimiu is dragged toward the club exit.

"Well!" Says Azgeviu. "It looks like you're going to have to find us another club now."

Rialdy said, "I have to go home. My girlfriend is expecting me. We're trying to conceive."

Azgeviu starts to protest, but Teoko puts a hand on his shoulder. "Let him go, he has a wife! We have to go get Frimiu in any case. They must have dumped him on the sidewalk."

The two Aranacians descend to the ground floor and head out the back exit to look for their friend.

Rialdy stays for one last drink.

4

A few weeks later, a tank disappears from Messel military base, at the foot of the Arachians mountain range. It's a training base, not as heavily armed or guarded as the strategic bases near national borders, but even so it's a first.

The military tries to put a lid on surrounding details. The tank is found abandoned the next day in the outskirts of a nearby town. By all indications, it's been abandoned due to running out of fuel. A runner out on an early-morning run passes in front of it and stops. The tank is sitting sideways in the roadside ditch, looking uncomfortable, as though it would like to fall over onto its side to rest. Surprised and amused, the runner climbs on top of the hulking behemoth. He raises his fists in the air, then feels slightly ridiculous. He takes a selfie with his phone. The pic appears on social media, then quickly moves to official media. The army hurriedly dispatches a retrieval team to get the tank back. Wary of minimizing media exposure, a heavy lift helicopter transports the tank back to base by airways.

The military have no jurisdiction to conduct the investigation of the theft off the base. They transfer all physical evidence they've gathered to the federal police department, while providing no details on how the theft could have taken place at all. The police have little to go on.

The physical evidence in question is a nylon back sack with a black plastic zipper that contains a gourd, a small multipurpose camping knife and a half-eaten apple. The police can collect no fingerprints or DNA from any of the articles. They throw away the half-eaten apple which has shriveled into a recalcitrant brown, wrinkled thing. Serial numbers on the back sack, gourd and camping knife are all traced to shipments having been made to Max and Tascha's camping goods store, Big Peak Outdoor Equipment.

Two policemen enter the store and approach Max, who peers at them from behind the counter. They identify themselves, show him the items, and ask to see all and any information he has concerning their sale. Max looks into his inventory. He has no record of having sold the items.

"That's strange," says Max. "They couldn't have been stolen from the shop because my inventory tells me they never left the storage. So whoever took them, took them directly from the storage room."

He stops. He realizes he may be incriminating Tascha. He abruptly shuts his mouth. Both policemen notice it immediately.

"Who has access to the storage room?" asks one policeman.

"Anyone," says Max. "Anyone can just come in. I leave it open. That's just the way I choose to conduct business. I want this place to be a place of trust, not one of those businesses where everything is locked away and everyone is suspect."

The policemen exchange a look.

"Can we take a look at your storage room?"

"You'll find it's locked today, actually." says Max. "It's exceptional. I don't like to follow principles too closely, not even my own. Makes you rigid. So today I locked the storage room."

"We'd like to see it."

The way they ask, Max doesn't know if he's allowed to say no, and there's no time to think about it.

"Of course," he says. "Just, you know, follow me or something."

He shows them the storage room, points to various camping products, asks them if they've ever camped and if there's anything they might be interested in that could take their camping experience to the next level.

"So," says one policeman, "you say you often leave the storage room unlocked. Is it possible that a customer could find his way back here without you noticing?"

"Oh, for sure. Sometimes when the product they need isn't in the front store I have them go into the storage room and take a look for themselves. There's an anti-theft system that detects products leaving the store through the front entrance but maybe people have a way around that. I can't always go with them to the storage room because I serve coffee at the bar too, and no one wants to wait for their coffee. I don't really have to worry much about theft, though. Most people who come to camp in these mountains have money, because it's a high-end nature town. Mostly draws well-to-do campers. But then, theft is a challenge and a pastime for some of these people, so I'm not surprised. I guess if someone is planning to steal a tank to go for a joyride, they won't stop at stealing a back sack or knife."

"Does anyone work here with you?"

"Just my girlfriend sometimes, but these days she rarely comes into the store. We're going through a bit of a rough patch at the moment. You know what it's like."

"We'd like to talk to her."

Max nods. "She's not here. I'd have to call her."

"We'll wait."

"I'll just call her."

"Please do."

"I don't get very good reception in the storage room. I'll just go back to the store if it's alright with you."

"We'll come with you. We've seen everything that we need to see here."

They head back to the front store. "I'll make you a coffee while you wait," offers Max.

He serves up two coffees and some cake. Dials Tascha's phone. The policemen chew on their cake, sip their coffee, never taking their eyes off Max.

"Tascha? I'm in the store and some men from the police department are here about some camping articles that came from our store. They were found on the scene of a theft."

"Why are you using your worried voice?" asks Tascha.

Max lowers his voice. "Yeah, so, they'd like for you to come over. It's about the theft of a tank?"

"The tank! I heard about that this morning. So hilarious. I'd love to do that, steal a tank and go for a joyride. Are they here about the tank?"

"Yes, they are here about the tank." Max gazes up at the policemen who are chewing in unison, jaws moving in circular motion. The movement is hypnotic and he can't wrest his eyes away.

"I'll be right over," says Tascha. "Make sure they don't leave until I get there. Why are you using your worried voice? It's not like you stole the tank. Did you steal the tank?"

"No," says Max.

He hangs up. "How's the coffee?"

One policeman nods and says, "Good."

The other policeman turns to the first one and says, "No, it's not. Why would you say it's good when you know it's not? How is this man supposed to improve the experience when you're giving him skewed feedback?"

"I'm being polite," protests the first policeman.

"This man doesn't care about your politeness," insists the other. "He's running a business here. He wants to improve the customer experience. Telling him the coffee is good when it's been made with hard water doesn't help at all."

"I don't give a shit," said Max. "Most customers don't give a shit either. And I can't do anything about the hard water. Tascha is on her way. Water is just the way it is, the way it comes to you. You can't change that."

Max sweeps the floors while the policemen wait for Tascha to arrive. He looks up at them now and then and admires how calm they look, staring around at camping equipment and sipping their coffees. They stand very straight, legs apart, thumbs of their free hands tucked into their belts. They stand like statues. They look like they could stand like that indefinitely.

Tascha walks into the shop and takes off her coat. She moves gracefully, like she's floating across the floor. She heads straight for the policemen and shakes their hands in turn, introducing herself.

"Max told me this is about the tank that went missing," she says. "We don't have it here."

"We need to ascertain certain facts about the people who have access to the storage room. That's where certain articles disappeared from that were found on the scene."

"No one has access to the storage except Max and I," said Tascha.

"Actually," says Max, "these past few weeks I've been leaving the storage unlocked."

Tascha turns to Max. "You leave the storage unlocked? Why would you do that?"

"Because you don't give a shit about the shop anymore, so why should I?"

One policeman clears his throat. "I can confirm that your boyfriend doesn't give a shit about the shop. This coffee, for instance, tastes burnt and is made from hard water. But I'd still like to know if the storage is left locked or unlocked, and whether or not you know anything about the back sack and knife that you see right over there on the counter." He leads Tascha to the counter. Tascha grasps the back sack and raises her eyebrows.

"Do you know this back sack?" asks the policeman.

"I...no. I mean yes, we bought a whole lot of these." she opens the back sack and takes a whiff. "Smells like apple."

"There was an apple inside when we found it."

"Was it half-eaten?"

The policemen share a look.

"Yes, there was a half-eaten apple inside. Why are you asking?"

Tascha shrugs. "That would explain how the apple smell is so strong inside."

The policemen stare at her silently a moment. Then one of them says, "If there's something you know about the apple, the back sack, the knife or the person who might have taken them from storage, you should tell us now. If you're holding back any information, that could prejudice you negatively for the remainder of the investigation. I don't need to tell you that the theft of military equipment is a serious offense, much more so than theft of private property."

"I don't know shit about the tank," says Tascha.

The policemen leave.

Tascha watches from the shop window as the police walk to their car. She waits until the car has pulled out and left the shop's street. Then, she laughs. A few snorts at first, then hiccups of laughter, then she a full-out guffaw.

Max chuckles a little too. "Funny, eh? About the tank being stolen?"

Tascha sits down on the shop floor, holding her sides. Her laughter has now become silent, contained, visible only through her shaking shoulders, tear-filled eyes scrunched closed.

"The back sack and knife though," says Max, "they really are from our storage room."

Tascha nods but can't stop laughing. She squeals.

"Did you take them, Tascha?"

Tascha nods again. Her laughter eventually subsides and she lies down on her back, sighing. "Yes, Max, I took the back sack and knife."

"Did you also take the tank?"

Tascha doesn't answer.

"Because," Max pursues, "it's pretty serious to steal a tank. It's not like stealing a back sack, you can go to jail, and it won't be a federal jail, it'll be a military jail."

Tascha gets up and dusts off the back of her jeans. She looked up at Max and says, "I didn't take the tank."

"Then how did the back sack and knife wind up in there?"

"Frin and I went camping. When we parted he kept the back sack and the knife."

"Frin." Max nods. "Why would Frin steal a tank? Frin doesn't do anything but groom himself and strut around town pursuing women."

Tascha shrugs. "You'd have to ask him."

...

Max lies on the couch trying to find sleep. He's gotten

used to the couch and enjoys its narrowness, the sagging middle, the arm rest where his feet lie, feeling the hardness of the wood underneath the armrest padding. None of his sheets fit the couch so he uses none. It feels like a temporary and unwelcoming shelter and he likes it that way. Every morning he wakes up with ankle pain from the wooden armrest edge digging into them.

His ears prick up when he hears Tascha descending the stairs. He sits up and looks at the staircase, expecting to see her in her bathrobe, but when her feet appear, then her legs, he sees that she's totally naked. Her body is dripping wet from the shower.

"Tascha?" He calls out. Tascha descends and reaches the floor. Her hair is dripping, drops pattering softly on the floor. She stands there a few moments, silently, looking for him in the dark.

"I'm on the couch," he says. His voice seems both too loud and not loud enough to reach her. It's like aiming a ball throw with voice volume.

Tascha moves slowly toward the couch. Her body glistens in the faint light filtering through the window. The scars on her legs are stark lines snaking up from her ankles to her hips and crotch. She's breathing quickly.

"What's going on?" says Max. "Couldn't find a tank to steal tonight?"

She says nothing. He wonders if she's really awake. He gets up from the couch to meet her.

She stops moving forward when she feels his touch. He guides her to the couch and sits her down. She immediately pulls her legs up and lies down on the couch, hands by her side. Her eyes are now closed again. Her muscles are tensed but her breathing is relaxing.

He lies down next to her and rests a hand on her stomach. Her skin is warm, still humid from the shower. He rubs his nose against her cheek.

"I've missed you," he says.

She turns her head toward him brusquely. He kisses her lips. He moves down to kiss her navel, then moves his head between her legs and breathes into her crotch until her legs part. He moves down and licks between the legs. Her body is now trembling. She puts a hand over her face and the trembling only increases. He realizes she's trembling not from desire but from sobbing.

"Tascha? What's going on?"

Tascha sobs. "Where are we, Max?"

"It's OK, we're in our home, we're on the couch."

"Why are we on the couch?"

"Because you kicked me out of the bed, like, weeks ago. Are you being serious right now? Tank joyriding makes you weird."

He sits up, glowering at her. She takes her hand off her face. She mouths a few silent words, then her voice finds her mouth, racked with fear. "What's happening to me, Max?"

He slumps forward on the far side of the couch, Tascha still taking up all the rest of it. He shakes his head. "I don't know, Tascha. Something's wrong with you, I'll admit that much."

"I'm scared, Max."

"What are you scared of? We live in a quiet touristy mountain town. We lack for nothing. We have friends. We go to church. There's nothing to be scared of."

"Maybe it's the memories, Max. Maybe they can come back even if they have no form to come back in. Maybe it makes them even harder to deal with."

"That's an interesting theory. We could put it to Doctor Tescar."

Tascha sits up. Max gazes at her naked body in the semi-darkness, the folds at her stomach, the long straight scar that goes from her neck down to the base of her back, the one scar that doesn't look accidental. It has a little wave in the middle of it, cruel and purposeful. He reaches out and traces it with a finger.

"Let's do that," says Max. "Let's call him up. He'll know."

They've had no contact with the Institute for the past few

years. There's been no reason to. They've been fine, adjusted, capable. Just like the other two Institute couples who live in the same town, who chose it along with them when the time came to leave the Institute.

Tascha nods, uncertainly. "What if I'm a freak? Maybe he can't help me. Maybe he won't even know where this goes."

"How about," proposes Max, "we talk to the others first? Maybe they're going through something similar and don't have words to put on it. Maybe they don't feel comfortable bringing it up, like a taboo. Let's have them over for supper this week, what do you think?"

Tascha nods, this time vigorously, almost childlike. "Yes," she says, "I'd like that."

5

They come to dinner. Baran and Sinvia, Gimel and Taltra, bearing bottles of wine and appetizers. Tascha welcomes them at the door and ushers them into the house.

"We haven't done this in too long, just meet up the six of us," says Sinvia as she plops down on the living room couch, patting the couch top in a proprietary way.

"I've always suspected it was part of our conditioning to want to avoid associating among ourselves," remarks Gimel. "We each have our one partner, that was supposed to be enough. The basic molecules of stability."

"Or," mutters Baran just loud enough, "maybe we just don't like each other very much."

Max pours wine for the guests and hands out the glasses. "It's been 17 years since we left the Institute," he announces. "In many ways, it's like we're all 17-year-olds living in thirtysomething bodies."

Gimel shakes his head. "We're not 17-year-olds. We have a memory cutoff from 17 years ago. It's not as though we started out from scratch. I, for one, feel wise. I know all of you think of me as the wise one." He lifts a glass in self-toast. Taltra slaps him over the shoulder. Wine spills onto the carpet.

"Oh!" exclaims Taltra, shocked and embarrassed. She puts her hands over her mouth as though she just said something vulgar and gross. "I'm so sorry, Tascha! I'll clean it up."

Tascha waves it off. "I don't care."

"That's Tascha's new thing, not caring," explains Max. "Tascha doesn't give a shit about anything anymore."

It's meant as a light barb but the bitterness shines through. A silence ensues. The guests exchange looks, taking the temperature.

"Thanks for that, Max," says Tascha. "That's actually what we wanted to talk to you all about. I've been going through some changes."

She looks around the room. Only Baran returns her stare. Sinvia, Gimel and Taltra look down. Max looks over at the wall.

"I know that you all know that Max and I haven't been together for a few weeks now. I was surprised that none of you came to ask me about it. None of you seemed to even wonder how it could happen."

"I asked Max about it, actually," says Baran, pointing toward Max as though there could be doubt which one was Max. "It's not that we're not interested, it's just none of our business." He shrugs. "Why would we worry anyways? You were a couple long enough, it did what it was supposed to, it got the job done, you can each move on the way normal people do when they break up."

"I haven't been myself lately," said Tascha. "I've been having strange dreams, violent, intense. I wake up in sweat. Sometimes I find myself somewhere and I'm incapable of accounting for the past few hours. I have exaggerated reactions to mundane events. I have sudden moments of hilarity and exhilaration."

"These are just normal things that people go through during breakups," offers Taltra. "It probably happens to everybody who breaks up."

"I called you here," says Tascha, "so we could think about how, after all these years, maybe our past is poking through the barriers that Doctor Tescar erected when we were at the institute. We've been living in suspended time, but that it may have finally caught up to us. I could just be the first to experience it."

Her words hang over them like a cloud.

"So what," mutters Sinvia,

"So what, Sinvia?" Says Tascha. "So what? We did things before we were reformatted. We did things that left permanent stains on our souls! This isn't about us being just a brain and neuronal pathways."

"Here we go!" shouts Gimel. "Here we go! You're bringing your religion into this when there's absolutely no reason for it. What if we don't have souls, Tascha? What if neuronal pathways are all that constitutes what we think of as our selves and we've been effectively reprogrammed? I'm sorry you and Max broke up, but the Institute people had no way of assuring us that we could stay coupled up for life. We were an experiment. Just go to the institute and tell Doctor Tescar that you've broken up. Maybe he can help you."

Tascha takes a large swig of her wine glass. "This is serious, and you're not see it."

"Tascha," says Taltra gently, "why do you think the old memories are bursting through? Maybe it's just your nature to be a slut and that's what's expressing itself after years of forced containment?"

Gimel points to Taltra, then points to Tascha, as if to transfer the opinion from one to another and buttress it. "She makes a good point, Tascha. What if you're just a slut?"

Tascha turns to Max. "Max, will you help me in the kitchen? Let's bring the food out."

Baran claps his hands together. "And let's have some music! We came here to party!"

Max accompanies Tascha to the kitchen, noting the tension in her neck and shoulders. He can hear Baran and Taltra arguing in the living room over what music to put on. He hopes Baran will win out so that the evening doesn't turn into couples dancing.

"Are you OK?" he asks Tascha in the kitchen.

"I'm fine," says Tascha, picking up a bowl of lentil salad. "My friends all think I'm a slut is all."

"Here," says Max, taking the bowl from her. "Let me get that."

Tascha looks lovely, with her hair done up on her head, wearing a dress that hangs down over her right shoulder. He'd like to kiss that shoulder. He'd try to if he wasn't holding the large bowl of lentils that makes it unfeasible.

He goes back to the living room, places the salad down on the buffet table against the far wall.

Tascha bursts into the living room, announcing, "You want proof? After I slept with Frin he went crazy. He left town and stole a tank. There's your proof. A tank! I did that to him. That's why we're arranged in couples, to keep our memories from contaminating other people!"

"I wish I had that effect on men!" shouts back Taltra. Baran has set the music to high volume and it's difficult to be heard. Taltra is swaying left to right, one hand holding her wine glass, her free wrist held in the air and turning over and over as though to urge the music to go on and not stop. She laughs. Max stands by the buffet table, watching the guests bounce around the living room floor. They haven't even eaten yet. They all arrived and went straight to dancing. There's been no catching up. They don't care that Tascha is deeply troubled, embroiled in her crisis.

But Tascha is now dancing along with the others. Unsmiling, wearing a grave and intense look, the kind she gets when she's focused on something technical, like when she's repairing a faulty product at the outdoor shop. Her movements are heavy, forceful. She approaches Baran, turns, and rubs her backside against his hip. Baran shakes his hips her way a few times before he looks up, sensing Max's glare. They remain a moment, Baran shaking his hips toward Tascha while he and Max lock stares. After a few moments, the eye contact makes Max doubt that he still inhabits his own body. He snaps himself out of it by throwing his hands up indignantly, popping his head forward as though to say 'What are you doing? That's is my wife!' Baran shrugs innocently, indicating Tascha's gyrating form with a hand, transferring to her the burden of guilt.

Tascha shimmies down and back up against Baran's side, oblivious to the exchange.

...

Max busies himself shuttling empty glasses and plates from the living room to the kitchen. He carries them one at a time to draw out the exercise, to allay the sinking feeling. Taltra joins him in the kitchen with an empty plate of her own.

"Did you know there's an orgy going on in this house?" asks Taltra. "Your wife is on the couch with Baran. Their clothes are coming off. Sinvia is straddling Gimel on the staircase. They could go upstairs, but they don't."

"Yeah, I noticed." Max keeps his back turned and washes dishes in the sink, letting the hot water scald his hands. The skin shows no sign of the heat he feels from the water.

'How much can we guess at that hides inside people?' he thinks.

He feels Taltra's hand on his upper back. "Why don't you join in, Max?"

He turns, leans against the sink. "This is crazy. Everyone is acting crazy. We can't do this. We don't have the emotional substrate to allow ourselves to —"

Taltra kisses him. She leans forward, puts her hands on his chest and connects her lips to his. He hesitates before responding in turn. Taltra smells like wine and a pungent perfume with notes of citrus and spice. Her shoulders are narrower than Tascha's. He grabs them and feels her heat through her loosely knit evening sweater. After a moment he pulls away, scrutinizing her, comparing her to Tascha. Her hair is longer, flatter. It hangs down over her shoulders, just above where his hands are now placed. He reaches up and flicks a strand of it.

"I don't want to go back into the living room if Tascha is there with Baran. I'll get the rest of the dishes later."

"We can just stay here, in the kitchen." She kisses him again. She whispers in his ear, "I like kitchens. I like the way I'm always pressing things and wagging casseroles around. A kitchen counter is the perfect height for sex. They should have kitchen counters in bedrooms. Pick me up, Max. I want to feel your arms flex to pick me up. I want to feel light and heavy at the same time."

Max picks her up. He swivels and places her on the counter. She reaches around him with her legs and pulls him in close. He puts his hands on her hips and kisses her, feeling her wrists on his shoulders and her hands in his hair. She has a physical way of claiming him in a way Tascha doesn't. He closes his eyes, emptying his mind of Tascha. Reaching down, he places his hands on Taltra's thighs and gives her a squeeze. She gasps and bites his lip slightly. Her hands move down to his shirt and pull it up, snaking underneath, moving across his back. He unfastens the front button of her jeans.

"Have you thought about this before, Max? You and I? Or did you really buy into the whole couples forever thing?"

Max chuckles ruefully. His own reaction surprises him and he feels silly. "I've never thought about this, sorry. I'm thinking about it now though. Is that OK?"

Taltra smiles coyly. "Let's not think."

She seems unhurried. Her husband is sitting on the staircase with someone else's wife. Max wonders if Gimel might have preferred Tascha and is staying nearby on the staircase within eyesight of her in case there's an opportunity for a quick switch.

He tugs on her jeans to peel them off. The tug reverberates throughout Taltra's form like a wave, ending at her head, a little jolt that she receives and yields to, still smiling, not breaking eye contact. He peels some more, gets down on his knees to pull the jeans down, around her ankles where they bunch against her heeled shoes. He flicks off the shoes, gets her jeans off. Her feet are unusually smooth for a woman who wears heels. He stands back up, presses himself against her. Her panties are plain, as though she dressed unprepared for the eventuality that someone other than her husband might see them tonight. Did this whole orgy just happen? Which one of them came to the party with thoughts of instigating it? He hopes it wasn't Baran. He hopes Baran is truly surprised at that he's on the living room couch with Tascha.

Taltra leans back on the counter. There's room enough behind her to place her hands. She looks as though she were reclining by the side of a swimming pool. She waits for him to remove her panties. She kicks a foot up as though an invisible doctor just tested her reflexes with a rubber hammer.

Max peels off her panties, bunches them up, holds them in one hand as he tries to take off his own jeans with the other, then drops them when his one-handed dexterity fails him.

When his jeans are off, he rubs his dick against her opening, drawing the wetness. He places his head beside hers, avoiding eye contact at this moment. He listens to her breathing, feeling the softness of her hair on his ear.

He enters her clumsily. Off-balance. Taltra reaches around her to steady herself and drops a bowl of cherries from the counter to the floor. The plastic bowl reverberates with a comical plastic thud. Cherries roll around in every direction.

He squeezes his eyes shut during the initial thrusts. He couldn't say if he were fucking Taltra or Tascha.

Taltra pulls his head away from her, pulling him by the hair. He thinks she looks angry, then realizes that's just her sex face. 'Sex transforms us all', he thinks. He wraps his arms around her waist and tries to pull himself toward her but she resists, holding his head away from her by his hair. It hurts. He likes it.

She moans suddenly, a single, isolated moan like a call. Her mouth remains open after it, panting.

One of his hands glances over the countertop between them. It's wet, from Taltra.

"I'm going to have to clean this counter afterwards," he says.

"Make me lick it," says Taltra. "Tell me to." He yanks her off the counter, spins her around and says 'Lick it. Lick the countertop. Make it clean, a place where you can prepare food.'

She licks it, big doglike, lapping licks. He waits a few licks, then enters her from behind. Her hair is straight. He'd been seeing Tasha's wavy hair for 17 years. Here he is now, fucking a woman with straight hair.

"Can you feel that?" he asks, his voice catching in his throat. "Can you feel me inside you? That's where I'm going to come. Right there. I'm going to come inside of you."

Taltra arches her back and turns to look at him, teasingly. 'Do it. Come inside of me. Do it now.'

He comes as if on cue. He gives a long, startled, pleading groan. She stares at him as he comes, panting. She smirks.

She pulls herself forward, letting him slip out of her. 'Let's go to the living room', she says. 'I want to watch the others.'

"No, I'm going to stay here." He stares down at himself, feeling suddenly silly again. Taltra puts her panties back on but leaves her jeans and shoes where they lie on the floor. She puts her arms around Max and kisses him softly.

"Come with me to the living room," she whispers.

"I'll just stay here. I still have dishes to do. I have to pick up these cherries."

Taltra deliberately steps on a cherry. The red flesh splays out under her foot, juice scattering. It looks like blood.

"Don't clean anything up," she says. "Don't get dressed."

"I'm going to get dressed."

Taltra looks pained. She embraces him tenderly, then makes her way to the kitchen door. She turns to him, pausing.

"Max, I have to say, I don't think Tascha is the one who is slipping away. I think you are."

Max pulls on his underwear and jeans, acutely aware of Taltra standing at the kitchen door awaiting his answer. He kneels on the floor and starts picking up the cherries, placing them in the plastic bowl.

Taltra lingers a moment, then pushes the door and disappears into the living room. In the brief instant that the kitchen door is open, he can hear the sound of Tascha moaning from the couch, and the lower, muffled sound of Baran's grunts.

He finishes picking up the cherries, puts the bowl back on the counter. He leaves the house through the back door, headed to the outdoor goods store to spend the night.

...

In the morning when he comes home, the guests have left. Tascha too.

She doesn't answer his texts.

6

Miles walks into the four person workspace, wearing his sunglasses. He double-points at Rialdy with each of his index fingers, from a slightly sideways stance.

"Heeey, guess what?"

Rialdy looks up and briefly wonders. Then he realizes.

"Oh. Did we get a contract?"

Miles nods in satisfaction. "You won't believe this, it's the Aranacians. I've never seen a sale go so fast. Went from prospecting to signing the contract in two weeks. Makes me look like a champion, but I suspect you deserve much of the credit. Where did you take them the other night? They signed this very morning! That must have been one spicy night."

"Tell me Miles, did you have the sunglasses ready in your office or did you bring them from home this morning?"

"I keep them around. Sometimes I put them on to feel confident. I'll wear them if I'm on the phone with a prospect. Call it a fetish."

"No, I don't think it's a fetish. sometimes we need a mask to show out true selves. This is you, Miles. this is the real you."

"There is something superhuman about sunglasses. The face remains recognizably human, but the eyes cannot be read."

Miles looks around, simultaneously acknowledging and announcing the awkwardness of his next question.

"Did you do anything, say... ethically unsound with the Aranacians? Because they're in the nuclear industry, so they're heavily linked to their government. If the sale was in any way influenced by illicit activities, ..."

"Yes?"

"Well, that would be bad. It'd be bad for everyone involved."

"I don't know what you're imagining but I'm genuinely curious. Anyway, I took them to a club. One of them got into a fight. I went home to conceive. I won't know if it worked for some time yet. I believe they continued to scout around for trouble. I don't think they got their fill with slamming just one guy on a club dancefloor."

Miles nods, still looking unsure.

"Well! If you weren't there for whatever followed, I guess it doesn't matter. We start implementing Monday at the client site."

"At the client site? Who's going?"

"You are, Rialdy my man. You're the star of this project."

"No, not me. Can't. Remember when I said I'm trying to conceive?"

"They asked for you personally. They insisted. Fact is, I was given to understand that it was a condition to the contract. They like you, Rialdy! It's an Aranacian thing, they like anything that comes from there."

"When you say, 'at the client site' —"

"Aranacia."

"Aranacia! I can't go to Aranacia! How long?"

"A month initially, but if all goes well we'll prolong it. You won't have to go for the full time, you just have to be there for the initial project, scope it out, develop the relationship, you know. You know how it is. They want a face they know, initially."

"Look Miles, I can't just leave my girlfriend here. We're trying to conceive a...a —"

Miles sits on his desk and puts a hand on his shoulder. "Look, Rialdy, if you do happen to get your girlfriend pregnant, what's her name again?"

"Tace."

"Tace, if you happen to get Tace pregnant, things'll change. You'll be spending all your time at home during the pregnancy, then afterwards caring for your child. There'll be no more travel, no more movement across land, no more of that foreign solitude in which a man finds himself. This is really your last chance to introspect in isolation, to get a sense of where you've been in life and where you're going. We're talking about Aranacia, the country where your mother came from. It's closing a cycle to your family history. Have you ever been to Aranacia? Are you at all in touch with your roots there?"

Rialdy feels Miles' hand on his shoulder oddly comforting. He tells himself that it's pure manipulation. He also finds that it works anyway. 'We're all just machines, programmable at will.'

He looks up. "Sorry Miles, can't do it. You're going to have to find someone else to go."

Miles gets up and goes to stare out the office window. The window sits above a coworker's desk, so Miles is standing very close to the man, peering right over his head. Uncomfortable, the coworker looks up at Miles, expecting him to leave. Miles ignores him and addresses Rialdy while facing the window over the coworker's head.

"I expected you might express this reticence, Rialdy. In any other circumstance I'd let you make that choice for yourself. We're not running a sweatshop here. We're all highly qualified and educated people who work best when given the leeway to make decisions and define our own parameters. But then, you have a contract, and the contract stipulates we can send you anywhere around the world, and we need you in Aranacia. If you break that contract, you can't take your niche talents elsewhere. Bla bla bla, you see where this is going. And I really wish you hadn't made me say it. This is on you."

Miles turns and walks toward the door. "I'll send you an email with the business documents and the plan," he says, before disappearing into the corridor.

Rialdy gets up to stand by the window. The co-worker sitting under the window gets up with a loud and petulant sigh.

"I'm going to take a coffee break. Enjoy the window view." He brushes brusquely past Rialdy. Rialdy pushes forward the empty chair and moves closer to the window.

...

He makes the mistake, that evening, of entering the house through the garage, to pick up his suitcase on the way in. Having his suitcase with him is tantamount to having already decided he's accepted the trip to Aranacia. Tace reacts to it immediately.

"What's that? You said over the phone we'd talk about this."

"We are going to talk about this," he fumbles. He scours his mind for an alternative explanation and comes up short. "It's just a suitcase." He sits down on the kitchen couch. "Come sit with me."

She stands, arms crossed. "This is about priorities, Rialdy. We're starting a family. This isn't the foot we want to start it on."

"It's just for a month."

"Really? How many of these encryption projects stick to the initial plan? You eventually find a whole stretch of legacy code that also needs encryption, then partner code, then they keep the consultants on for good measure. 'If something needs to be protected, then everything needs to be protected.' You say that yourself. Why are you —"

Tace stops and leans her forehead against the fridge door. "Why would you even say that this is just for a month? You don't believe it yourself. You're talking to me like I'm the client you need to bullshit."

Rialdy springs up hurriedly from the couch and goes to comfort her. He's aiming to enlace her, assuage her, but he imagines she'll push him away and he shrinks from the probability. He stands near her with his hands in his pockets.

"Look, if this were any other job, I'd just quit and go elsewhere. But this is my niche and if I quit I have nowhere to go. I have a non-compete clause. They can make me leave the whole field."

"Fine then. If you have to. If there isn't a choice."

She makes his suitcase for him. He refuses at first,

wanting to do it himself, then relents when she insists. He thinks it might feel as though they'd come to this decision together. Now, as he stands in the bedroom watching her pack, it feels like she's throwing him out of the house in a leisurely way, taking her time and enjoying the prospect of it.

Tace packs everything tight, getting in as many clothes as possible. Rialdy shifts uneasily from one foot to another, hands in his pockets. She doesn't appear to take any notice of him as she packs. When she omits his fetish pair of jeans, he thinks to tell her but doesn't, not wanting to interfere, not wanting to appear as though with his fetish jeans packed in his suitcase he'd have no reason to come back.

When it's done she sits on the bed and finally acknowledges him. She clasps her hands in her lap.

"Do you want to try? Before you leave?"

There's nothing enticing about the way she is sitting, with rounded back, in her sweatpants and fluffy grey socks. She looks pained when he doesn't answer immediately. "Never mind."

...

That Saturday evening, they have supper at their regular restaurant. They eat slowly, wanting to prolong the moment.

"I'm going to miss this," say Rialdy. When Tace looks up sharply from her plate he realizes how it must have been perceived and laughs nervously. "That came out wrong." Tace doesn't answer.

...

On Monday morning he wakes up at 5:00 a.m. to get to the airport. Tace gets up with him and fixes breakfast. Rialdy is excited, trying to hide it and failing. He looks at his watch too much. His gaze darts around the kitchen. His head bobs to a song he's playing mentally. He doesn't dare whistle it but he gets the melody going in the faintest way possible just by blowing out softly while shifting his tongue around in his mouth.

"Won't you be coming home before the contract ends?"

asks Tace. "Like, every two weeks or so? You said it's a lucrative contract, right? You could insist that they pay for trips home."

Rialdy shrugs. "Not sure it's worth doing for just a month's intervention." He's just repeating the half-truth about the intervention only lasting a month. He sighs but doesn't rectify.

"Do you want to try? One last time before you leave?"

"Now?"

"If you have time."

"I don't. I have to get to the airport."

"OK.

"I'm sorry."

"It's OK."

...

As the taxi pulls away from the house he turns and watches it recede. He imagines how, decades ago, his mother must have watched a house like it recede in Aranacia.

...

The plane takes off from Tradot airport, veers north then north-east-east, reaches the Atlantic, soars over Iceland. Sometime before reaching Aranacia the ride becomes turbulent, awakening Rialdy in the middle of a dream in which he'd been following the instructions of a disembodied, cackling voice guiding him as he ran through an urban landscape in perfect darkness. The dream is imbued with some kind of emotional, musical realization that he struggles to retain in the midst of the shaking. When the turbulence subsides, he finds he can recall nothing of the dream but vague images of the urban landscape. It makes him wonder how he could remember any images at all if he'd been running in perfect darkness.

The plane lands in Aranacia's main airport. Rialdy hops on a bus to Aranacia City's central train station. He takes the first train headed for the western tip. From there he takes a special bus that crosses the almost kilometer-long bridge which is the only passage to the island of Wizniu.

Wizniu, a historically semi-autonomous island, has a set of laws that allows for businesses to set up and avoid paying taxes. The bus stops on the other side of the bridge and is boarded by customs agents, who inform Rialdy that they'll be keeping his passport for the length of his stay on the island. When he protests, they insist that it's a condition for entering the island, no exceptions for foreigners, but he can reclaim it any time he should wish to leave. He hands it over to them reluctantly, receiving in return a temporary visa stamped with his passport information.

From the bus station he takes a taxi for Rare Earths Mining Plant, which is built so close to the sea that it appears to be sinking into it. The taxi leaves him on a dirty beach a few hundred meters from the plant, which looms high on his approach. Windblown sand sifts into his shoes, ruffles his hair. He tries to pat it down before entering the building.

Inside, he approaches the reception desk, introducing himself as a representative of Empiricole, saying he's expected. The receptionist asks for him to leave his identification papers, which he hands over with an irritated gesture.

"I'll have no personal identification papers so long as I'm here!" he snaps. The receptionist stares back at him blankly a moment, then replies, "You can have your papers back whenever you leave the mining plant."

He waits in the lobby for Azgeviu. Azgeviu arrives, smiling and chipper. He apologizes that Teoko and Frimiu won't be joining them. He proposes a coffee at the plant café, where the luxurious wooden and brass bar is at polar odds with the plant's drab, worn, functional setup. They're served Aranacian smoked coffee. Azgeviu winks at him.

"Smoked coffee is an acquired taste. When you finish your stay here you'll probably like it so much you'll import it to Canada."

Rialdy sips the coffee and grimaces.

"It tastes like, well, the taste, reminds me of... smoked salmon. I guess it's a taste I just don't associate with coffee."

"In Aranacia, we smoke everything. If it isn't smoked, it's doused in additives that mimic the taste of smoked food. Apparently it's a cause of cancer. New cancer studies come out all the time. They contradict one another endlessly."

Azgeviu speaks to him in English, as does anyone in the plant addressing him. Rialdy would have liked to practice his Aranacian but wants to retain any linguistic advantage he might have in English so long as he's functioning in a professional setting.

They take the elevator and descend far below ground level. Rialdy blanches a little upon entering the elevator when Azgeviu presses the button to minus 50.

"How safe is the structure of the plant? Isn't part of the building immersed in the sea?"

Azgeviu shrugs. "It's safe. We have never had any problems at this plant. In any case, if the sea were to gobble up the building, it would change nothing if you were above ground level or below it. It would all go down."

Azgeviu takes him into a one-person office where he'll be working in the upcoming weeks. Azgeviu boots the computer, perched on an old wooden desk that looks as though it's been designed for an overgrown child.

"The code base is all here in a folder we have prepared for you. You have to make a list of tools that you need installed on the computer for your work. Someone from the IT department will come and install them for you. Do not to hesitate to ask any question that you might have."

Azgeviu nods and leaves.

Rialdy settles into work for a few hours. When he looks up at the time it's already 8:00 p.m. The entire trip from Montreal to Wizniu took twelve hours. Now, in an office by himself, disconnected from the work cycle of the other workers in the plant, he's lost his time bearings. He feels no hunger. He wanders out of the office and into the hall. The lights are out. He scours the wall for a light switch but finds none. Where are light switches set in Aranacian buildings? The plant is an old structure, they can't very well be automated. He goes back into the office and lights his desk lamp, then back into the hall to see how far the light projects. Disappointed, he switches it off, grabs his suitcase and makes his way down the hall toward the elevator, dragging a hand along the wall, feeling the cold, rugged surface tug at his skin. Now and then he spots pilot lights, little red diode-like points blinking from the ceiling.

The elevator is shut down for the evening. He presses the button over and over, thinking it might reactivate, with no result.

He pushes open the stairwell door and makes his way up to the ground floor. In the dark, he can focus on little else than his labored breathing as he walks up, two stairs at a time, then one, all 50 floors. His suitcase rolls over and bumps against the steps, jolting his arm. He emerges, exhausted and panting, in the lobby. Light, finally. The day receptionist has been replaced by the night receptionist, a young woman with a name tag, 'Eva.' She looks up at him in wonder as he approaches.

"Where did you come from?" she asks, in English. He wonders how it could be so obvious that he's not from around here.

He stands at the desk and holds up a finger, waiting to catch his breath. "I'm a consultant from Empiricole. I was working. I lost my sense of time."

Eva nods, waiting for more, smiling encouragement. She's wearing heavy eyeliner. It seems at odds with nighttime duties.

"Does anyone work here in the evenings?" asks Rialdy. The question seems to make her uncomfortable.

"Meetings are held here in the evenings."

"I need a cab to get to my hotel." He produces the information from his pocket on a printed-out email. She takes it from him, sets it out on the desk, presses it out to remove the creases. "You're staying at the Highest Comfort?"

"Yeah."

She shoots an eyebrow up. "Fancy." Then she looks back

down at the paper, fixating on the hotel name.

"Well, I don't pay for it," says Rialdy.

"Then I guess we do."

"Can you get me a cab?"

She doesn't answer for a moment, still fixating on the hotel name. "I'll take you there myself, much easier. The cab will overcharge you."

"I bill everything. I don't even look at the price. I can't ask you to abandon your post."

She shakes her head. "I'll take you there. Much easier." She remains there waiting, hands clasped in front of her on the desk.

"Shall we go?" He points to the exit door, as though to make sure that's the way out.

Eva nods. "I just need to leave a note for anyone who might come in." She takes a piece of paper, writes a few lines, folds it and sets in on the reception desk in front of her. It stands there, in a stable triangular structure. Eva grabs her bag and walks around the desk.

"Won't you get fired?"

She laughs. "No. Let's go. I have a car."

They leave the building. There are few lights in front of the building. The sound of the waves from the sea waft in through the dark. Eva's is the only car in the parking lot.

As they drive away from the plant, she turns on the radio.

"So, the address is —"

"I don't need the address. I know where the Highest Comfort is."

'She's been there before.' From the passenger seat he observes her receptionist clothes, the skirt, the well-pressed jacket, the square shoulders. Her hands and painted fingernails. He imagines her meeting someone at the Highest Comfort. A consultant like himself?

She pulls into a street in Wizniu's urban center. There are hotels, restaurants, bars, a denser network of light posts. She parks the car in front of the hotel.

"Well," said Rialdy. "Thanks for the lift."

"I'll come inside with you. It's not given that the person

at the desk speaks English.”

“I speak some Aranacian. My mother was —”

Eva has already opened her door and gotten out. They walk into the hotel, Eva a few steps ahead, Rialdy wheeling his suitcase. She heads straight to the front desk and engages the front desk man in lively Aranacian, too fast for Rialdy to follow. He recognizes only his name. She retrieves the key and turns to Rialdy. “Fourth floor.” She moves toward the elevator and beckons for him to follow.

He hesitates, joins her. They go up to the fourth floor, avoiding eye contact. Eva moves briskly to the room, beeps open the door with the key card and steps in. Rialdy follows, his suitcase silent on the room’s carpet. He sets it against the wall, removes his portable computer case and placing it on the desk. Eva stands in the middle of the room, looking at the bed, looking at the desk. She goes into the bathroom and stands there a moment, running a finger along the edge of the sink. She comes back into the room. Sits down on the bed.

Rialdy lets himself fall into the desk chair, turning it around to face Eva. His legs are tingling. His heart is racing. He clears his throat.

“So, Eva. Where did you learn to speak such good English?”

Eva smoothes the bed’s top cover with a hand. “I studied a year in America.”

“I’m from Canada.”

“I know that.”

“Our English is a little different. We pronounce things a little differently.”

“If you say so. I can’t hear it in your speech.”

Rialdy nods. “I’ll only be in Aranacia for a month.”

“Well, a month is not too short for having fun. If you’re looking for some fun things to do in the evenings, there’s a bring-your-own-culture night in a bar not far from here that you might enjoy. I go there every Wednesday. It’s a good break from the weekly grind. I almost never miss it. Why don’t you come this Wednesday?”

"I don't really have any culture to bring."

"Then just come to listen. You should hear me sing. I've been told that I have an expressive voice." She says it frankly, holding his gaze.

"That could be fun." He shifts uneasily in his seat, trying to read the moment's undercurrents, trying to read her signs.

As though suddenly aware of his scrutiny, Eva laughs and briskly pats the bed with both hands. "Well!" She stands up. "I'll be getting back to my desk. Some people arrive after 11:00 p.m. I have to be there when they come in, even though they'll just walk past my desk."

"Miners?"

"No. Decision-makers. The miners only work during the day. And they don't arrive through the front entrance. They come from underground. Some of them come from the sea lift. That's how it's been since the war. Aranacia hid its mines in plants to shield them from aerial view."

She pauses. "That's a good description of the Aranacian psyche, too. Aranacians hide themselves from aerial view. We are really visible only to the people who are stuck at our level." She shrugs. "You'll probably be gone before you have a chance to see Aranacians the way we see ourselves. You will remain with your aerial view."

"Like a bomber."

"You don't look like a bomber to me. You look more like a cargo that's been dropped from above, that's swaying left and right on its parachute ropes, descending toward the ground, probably bound to get stuck in the branches of a tree. I say that in a good way, don't get me wrong."

"It's strange though, that technical and engineering services should be in the same building as the mine, isn't it?"

"I see you've already gotten stuck in the branches. I'll be going now." She walks over to the desk, bends toward him and kisses his cheek, then pats it like an old friend. "See you at the plant or at the bring-your-own-culture night. You should hear me sing. My voice has been compared to a flowing stream."

"A what?"

"Someone I once knew said that." She looks around the room. "Well!" She says. She leaves, closing the door softly behind her.

Her scent lingers in the room. Rialdy grows restless, debating whether to call Tace. He decides to postpone it until morning.

He unfolds the hotel room ironing board and irons out his shirts out before hanging them in the closet along with his vests. He shines his shoes. He opens a mini bottle of whiskey from the minibar and sips from it while writing an email to Miles to report on his appreciation of the work load. He holds the bottle between his teeth, no hands, tipping his head back to drink. The bottle has an impossibly small opening, that he can slip the tip of his tongue into. When he pulls his tongue back, a few drops slip into his mouth. As he types the email he throws his head back every few words. The bottle is empty before he finishes the email. He opens his mouth and lets it fall into his hands. It slips through his fingers and clatters against the edge of the chair before falling to the floor.

7

Guide Erek is delivering his sermon in church. Max cranes his neck over the seats, searching for either Frin or Tascha. Extrapolist Church adherents don't have regular seat. Seating is random, buttressing the notion that no soul is locked to any one place in the universe and that people-souls find themselves through travel and interaction. To Max, this is unsatisfying. An absent person should produce an absent seat. Absence is its own kind of presence.

After the sermon, he speaks with Guide Erek in the church basement.

"Tascha's gone."

Guide Erek nods. "She probably followed Frin."

"That makes sense."

"I know where Frin went, by the way."

Max frowns. "Guide Erek... Should you be volunteering that kind of information?"

"I can because when Frin told me, he'd just offered me a beer. So that transformed our conversation into, not a spiritual asking of guidance, but rather just two buddies having a beer."

"I'm curious. When did the conversation just magically transform itself? Was there a moment right after he'd handed you the beer and you hadn't yet grasped it and you were partly in a guidance session and partly in beer talk?"

"That's a question for higher guides than myself. I'd say it became beer talk when he offered me a beer and I accepted. Beer itself is just a symbol."

"What if it'd been tea? Or a glass of water?"

"Then I'd still be bound by the sacred act of the Guide-Traveler sharing. For sure."

"What about Irish coffee? The coffee helps you keep

awake, but then boom, you get a shot of whiskey with it."

"Definitely a friendly conversation if there's whiskey involved."

Max nod, lets a moment pass to signify deep respect for Guide Erek's teaching. "So where did Frin go?"

Erek doesn't answer immediately, still puzzling about the beverage enigma regarding Guides and Travelers. When he does reply, his voice is animated, gleefully basking in one of those rare moments when he can betray a Traveler's confidence with impunity.

"You won't believe this, Max. Frin went searching for Tascha before Tascha'd even left you. He went looking for Tascha's past. In his own words, after they slept together he felt he could had been infected by her, by some soul contamination that Tascha might have been carrying but was immune to, and you too, of course. He thought that, like a local dweller on an isolated continent, he'd been contaminated by immigrants who've lived in promiscuity for centuries and developed immunities to all sorts of diseases that they've forgotten about but nevertheless still carry."

"That's fucked up."

"As you say."

"Is it even possible? Can a soul be infected with a disease?"

"I imagine it can. Everything is code, Max. The universe is composed of a multitude of different machines that obey its laws acting in accordance to some code. A virus is just a bit of code that latches itself onto one such machine. Our bodies build themselves according to our dna. People at work take instructions from other people. The soul assembles code from each passage through material existence. When Frin told me he'd been infected by Tasha, I couldn't say how it happened, technically, but I could see in his tone and his gestures that he wholly believed it. His mind is full of images of Tascha's past. He intends to follow those images wherever they lead."

Max looks pointedly at the Guide. "So, Tascha is

following Frin, and Frin is following Tascha?"

Guide Erek nods. "That's what I think. Frin and Tascha are on a loop. They are intertwined." Erek makes a gesture with both hands, pressing each thumb to the index finger of the other hand.

"Tell me how to find them."

"I don't know how to find them. Are you going to try to get Tascha back?"

Max nods. "I want her back."

"I have to say, Max. I don't think you're even a part of this equation. You're not in the loop."

"How dare you! That's my wife you're talking about!"

"Wife, friend, Guide, all these roles are temporary, Max. The role has its own life, and then it dies, and if we try to hang onto it after it's dead, it's like holding onto a calcified mummy. Don't get me wrong, I acknowledge your attachment, and if you feel that you must go after her, then go after her."

Max nods.

"Be aware of one thing, though." Guide Erek holds up a finger, arching his eyebrows. As he does this Max notices that he's now giving the Guide his full attention. The Guide exhibits such an aura of confidence in what he knows, manifests so little doubt, that Max can't help but want everything he says to be true.

"What?"

"Even if you think you are, you're not necessarily following Tascha."

...

Max hypothesizes that Tascha might be camping with Frin again. He hikes up the mountain, following the paths they used to take together, looking for some trace. He pauses now and then to shout her name at the top of his voice. "Tascha! Taschaaaaaa!"

He considers shouting Frin's name too, but he doesn't want to give the bastard the satisfaction of hearing his name called out.

He wanders over the mountain, going over the regular

camping spots and also the hidden ones, the ones known only to hikers very familiar with the mountain.

"Taschaaaaaaa!"

He does this for a few days.

He doesn't know what he'd do if he did find her tent. Just wait in front of it and call out her name? Peer inside, risking finding her enlaced with Frin, sharing a sleeping bag?

He doesn't know where to look for her if it's not on the mountain. This is their place, the place they used to go to rekindle their sense of self.

After a few days, his voice is hoarse from shouting. He knows that he's known, from the start, that she's not here.

He climbs to the peak of the mountain. At the top, the wind blows softly in the warm afternoon sun. He looks out over the surrounding landscapes, feeling the sun warm his neck and back.

On the plains below he can see villages. He can see roads on which minuscule cars and trucks snake along. He can see electrical lines. He takes it all in, and it hits him: he has only to check the online statements of the joint bank account he shares with Tascha to know where she is.

...

In Aranacia City. She's been frequenting a café every morning, paying 12.50 araks each time. Max figures it's about twice the price of a coffee, so she's probably paying for that wife-fucker Frin too. Financed by his own hard work in the outdoor shop.

...

He rents a van to make the trip to Aranacia City, a spacious vehicle in case Tascha has bought furniture that needs to be transported home after he'll have persuaded her to come back.

He hasn't driven in years. It's been a source of pride, being able to live in a secluded mountain environment without owning a motorized vehicle, living with a minimized carbon footprint. But now, it feels good to drive. He feels powerful. He drives with the radio on full blast, loud enough to hurt his ears, tuning in to hard rock stations. He pummels the dashboard as he drives, often letting go of the steering wheel, head banging to the music.

At a gas station, he buys a pair of mirrored sunglasses, with a coating that gives off rainbow-colored glints. He gets a haircut, short in the back and on the sides, long on top, hanging down sideways over his forehead.

The drive to Aranacia City takes three days. During this time he doesn't change his clothes. He sleeps in the van.

He finds the café, a nondescript place. The surroundings are somewhere between residential and commercial. There are shops and cafés around. He parks the van in front of the café and spends the day wandering around the district. It's frequented by a young crowd, and after some time observing their bright clothes and weird fashion statements it dawns on him that it must be a student district, that there must be a university nearby.

He finds it nestled in a block with an even denser network of cafés. He stands in front of the entrance, the tall brick wall and the towering sign, 'Aranacia National University 6'. He knows who he'll find here. He heads in to the front desk and asks for directions to Doctor Tescar's office.

...

Doctor Tescar looks up when he walks in. He doesn't recognize him until Max removes the sunglasses.

"Ah, Max! I knew you'd find your way here eventually. Please sit down. You must be looking for Tascha."

Max sits in the chair facing the desk. "So you know about our breakup."

Doctor Tescar nods. "Sorry to hear about it. How're you holding up?"

Max looks down at his hands. "It's hard, Doctor Tescar. I thought we couldn't separate. I thought we were bound by a mathematically proven model. You showed me the equations, remember?"

Doctor Tescar shrugs, chuckles. "Oh, that. The model was flawed. It worked the first year of the program, then it didn't work at all the following years. Our funding was cut after the third year of showing statistically unmeaningful results. I left the institute, found a place here." He gestures toward the walls and out the window.

"I don't know what we did right that year. But, the first batch of recycled child soldiers was the only one for whom it worked, forming long term romantic partners that built off of their shared amnesia."

"About that, I was wondering. A few of us Institute couples were wondering, in fact, if our memories might be coming back, those that came before our treatment."

Doctor Tescar shrugs. "It could happen. It might not. You know, the human psyche is profoundly resilient. I mean, you were child soldiers and you were forced to witness and perpetrate incredibly violent acts that led to traumatic effects on your psyches, but that's the way mankind has always lived, the constant threat of imminent violence. Walk with me, Max, there's somewhere I need to go."

They leave the office, head down a flight of stairs, cross a large courtyard bordered with plants and abstract art works. Doctor Tescar appears engrossed in his thoughts and Max grows ever more curious as to what the doctor has planned to show him. When they enter the lobby of the community building, however, he sees that the doctor is just headed for a vending machine. Doctor Tescar feeds some change into a slot and waits avidly for a bag of potato chips to roll forward on a spiral screwlike dispensing rod.

"Do you want something?" asks Doctor Tescar. "My treat."

Max shakes his head.

"Let's go back into the courtyard," says the doctor.

"I have to tell you, Max," says Doctor Tescar as they emerge back into the sunlight of the courtyard. "I was a young researcher in human resilience and I was working on a theory that human couples can heal one another. I didn't see the politics of it. Forces in the government at the time seized upon my theories to set up a treatment center for war refugees. When you're young, you think you see all the cons, but you only see the ones you thought would be there in the first place. I was totally blindsided by the government's agenda. But then, it was so intoxicating to have such support that I suppose I willfully shut my eyes to that agenda."

The doctor has finished eating his chips. He drops the empty bag to the ground.

Max stares at it, startled. "Aren't you going to put that in the garbage?"

Doctor Tescar shrugs. "Someone will pick it up. It's work for the cleaning crew."

Max watches the empty chips bag float slowly away, then kick up into the air when a slight breeze hits it.

"So, what I'm getting at," says Doctor Tescar, "is that the goal of the program wasn't really to get bad memories out of child soldiers. It was more a way of culturally isolating refugees as much as possible, to transform them into proper Aranacians before letting them into Aranacian society. It was a kind of ethnic cleansing."

"Oh." said Max. "Wait - we weren't Aranacians originally?"

Doctor Tescar stops walking and stares directly at Max. "Look at yourself, Max. Your features aren't Aranacian. Ditto Baran, Tascha, Symbia —"

"— Sinvia —"

"Whatever, none of you look Aranacian. Haven't you figured that out by yourselves yet? How could it escape your attention?"

Max takes off his sunglasses, flips them over and stares at himself reflected on the right lens. His reflection is deformed, his nose impossibly large, his head flattened at the top and at the chin. It would appear comical to him if he weren't scrutinizing his reflection for signs of extra-Aranacian origin.

"I don't know," says Max in a guarded tone. "You tell me Doctor Tescar. You're the one who conducted the washing up of our identities. You're the one who rebuilt us."

"Rebuilt, yes. But that's such a loaded word. I don't know what I did right that first year of the program, but whatever it was, it worked. And then it didn't. There was something there, an added parameter that disappeared when we moved the institute to Aranacia City. It must have been something in the air. But how do you isolate that kind of parameter?"

"Where was the old institute?"

"In Terrytown. We needed space near to the refugee camps, and all we found was the old Biosphere Evolution Laboratory."

"Terrytown. Is that where we were? The name seems familiar and distant at the same time."

Doctor Tescar chuckles. "No. You know it because of the Terrytown zoo. Hey, Max? I'm sorry to hear about your separation. But, you know, you don't seem haunted by memories of your war-torn past, so, you know, move on. The others didn't even get that, those fifteen years of blissful domesticity. And, I don't think they're as integrated in Aranacian society today as you are."

"Doctor Tescar, I have to say it. You're a bit of an asshole. I didn't remember you as such when you were treating us."

"That's what Tascha said to me. People change, Max."

"Tascha was here?"

"She was. She was with another guy, tall, good-looking. Max, really. Move on."

Max waits in the courtyard as Doctor Tescar disappears through the door at the far end, headed toward the stairs leading to his office.

He waits there a few minutes, then turns and heads back toward the community building. He spots the empty chips bag, fluttering gently at the foot of a statue. He approaches it. A gust lifts it off the ground as he approaches and carries it a few meters away. He takes a few running steps and steps on it hard, before picking it up and throwing it into the nearest garbage can.

8

Rialdy stares at the computer screen in his one-person office. The onscreen code has been blurring before his eyes. The comments in Aranacian are increasingly hard to decipher. He checks the time: 8:30 p.m., shuts down the computer and heads out to the elevator. He now knows how to activate it after hours, but the corridor lights are controlled from a room that remains locked in the evening, so he walks in darkness, hand trailing against the wall to his right.

Eva is at the reception desk when he emerges into the lobby. He stops by, leaning against the counter.

"Well, I'm done," he says. "I don't know about you."

She looks up. "I'm here for a while still." Looks back down at her book.

He nods, stands there, uncertain.

"What are you reading?" he asks, not willing to exit just yet.

"It's a god story," she says. "Typical Aranacian genre. They don't sell these outside of Aranacia. I don't think they've even been translated. There's no point, I suppose. No market. No gods, probably." She laughs.

As she makes eye contact, he sees she was waiting for him to ask.

"So, this bring-your-own-culture night, where does it take place?"

"Not far from your hotel, actually. I'll write down the address for you. Will you be there tonight?"

"It's Wednesday. You said it takes place every Wednesday, so I thought I might. But you're working tonight, so I guess you won't be going?"

"I might make it anyway. It generally goes on until late."

She scrawls the address and hands him the paper. "Go there," she says. It's more than a recommendation. It's said in a quiet voice but unmistakably a command. He folds the note, slips it in into the front pocket of his jacket and nods. "I might. I might go. I don't know, I'll see." He nods. "Well!" His voice is overly cheerful.

She smiles, goes back to reading her book.

...

He phones Tace from the taxi. He's given the taxi driver the address and not that of his hotel.

"Hey babe. I just left work, on my way back to the city. Just a slog day, recoding for hours. Talked to no one. Must have said maybe a dozen words today, just to get my lunch tray and pay. That's it."

Tace is busy cleaning, but attentive nevertheless. "Do you have plans for the evening?"

"No, just catching up on my sleep."

"You haven't been sleeping?"

"Oh, I've been sleeping, but the work is so demanding, I'm exhausted in the evenings."

"Maybe you should get out, have some fun." she pauses. "Tell me, where exactly was your mother from, in Aranacia?"

"I don't know. She may have mentioned Aranacia City, but she never really dug into any kind of detail on the matter. Or maybe she did and I forgot. Maybe she was born there but lived elsewhere. I always got the feeling she wanted to let go of it all, that she didn't want me to be bound to a country that she herself had left behind."

"Well. She spoke to you in her mother tongue. There has to be some kind of attachment in that."

Rialdy feels a knot in his chest. He knows he'll buy cigarettes sometime that evening.

"It doesn't matter."

"How could it not matter? Especially now, with us, now that we're starting a family?" The tension is mounting in Tace's voice.

"Well, if you like, you can join me in Aranacia and spend

your days researching my mother's origins while I work. I really don't have time."

"Would you like that? For me to join you there?"

"How's that possible? You're working. You can't just up and join me here."

"I could take time off work. I'd be up for it."

"You wouldn't see me at all. I'm working all the time."

"But would you want it? If I could, would you want me to join you in Aranacia?"

"I don't know. Yes, yes I would. But it's not feasible."

"OK."

There's a silence.

"Sorry, I'm just tired."

"Rest up. I'm thinking of you."

"Me too." He catches the taxi driver looking at him in the rearview mirror as he hangs up. He stares back, wondering how much of his conversation the man has overheard. The driver turns back to the road ahead.

...

Girali's bar is very close his hotel. He realizes he's passed by it a few times on his evening walks while looking for places to eat. He eats out every evening, taking full advantage of being able to bill it. He orders entrees and desserts that he doesn't finish, sometimes that he scarcely even picks at. He leaves whole plates half-finished. He feels a perverse satisfaction in wasting food.

The bar is lit through a series of small spotlights set in the ceiling in no particular order or alignment, haphazardly. Rialdy get a beer at the counter and asks the bartender if the spotlight arrangement represents a constellation or something else. The bartender replies that it's probably just decorative. Rialdy nods eagerly as though it were some kind of revelation. He turns around with his beer surveying the bar with a wide I-totally-fit-in smile before heading to a free table, bobbing his head to the bar music.

People entering the bar head straight to a man sitting by the wall who writes down their names in a little book, ostensibly the evening's list of performers. The man eventually closes the book and goes to stand on a small stage, asking for the audience's attention before welcoming everyone and saying a few words about the event. He introduces the first performer who takes the stage timidly, reciting a poem. Rialdy finds, as he gazes at the poet recite, that he's incapable of focusing on any of her words. After a few moments he lets his mind drift and occasionally glances toward the door, watching for Eva.

The performers come and go, succeeding one another in different performance arts: poetry, song, magic tricks. One man does acrobatics even though the stage is too small to accommodate it. The bartender protests that he'll end up breaking something if he continues. The host assures him he knows the acrobat personally and has seen him perform in even more confined spaces. The bartender, unconvinced, nevertheless turns reluctantly to head back to the bar.

Predictably, the acrobat loses balance on a handstand and pitches forward, taking down a table, two bottles and five empty glasses with him. It happens the instant the bartender turned his back, so it seems rehearsed. Rialdy laughs along with the rest of the bar as the bartender comes right back and berates the host vociferously. The host turns to the audience to announce a twenty minute break. Rialdy, already feeling the onset of drunkenness, gets a pack of cigarettes from a dispenser in the men's washroom. Such machines have long since disappeared in Canada. It feels quaint to push coins into the slot and punch the code for the pack. He smiles as the pack comes tumbling down to the windowed opening.

Outside, he lights up and waits for the head-spinning sensation. Cigarettes make him slow down, as though the air around him were growing suddenly thin, weakening him head to foot, making him dizzy, making him want to sit down. In contexts like this, standing outside, he feels as though the smoke he's blowing connects him to the people around him, announcing his presence, inviting human interaction.

An older man comes up to him. "You look like

somebody's boyfriend," he says, in English. "Is your girlfriend performing tonight?"

Rialdy laughs. "I'm nobody's boyfriend. Not here, anyway."

"Does that mean you're performing? If you're not performing, you're somebody's boyfriend. You're one or the other."

"Nope." Rialdy blows some smoke rings upwards. The night is cool. A breeze blows through his work shirt and he realizes he's left his jacket inside along with his laptop. He peers inside the bar through the front window. There's a man holding his laptop up to eye level, as though weighing it. He runs inside.

"Hey!" he snaps. The man turns around, unhurried. It's the host.

"This laptop is really light," says the host.

Rialdy reaches forward and takes it from him.

"I wasn't going to take it," explains the host. Rialdy turns to give him a pointed stare and places the laptop back at the foot of his table.

The host thrusts a hand forward. "I'm Fimandi."

Rialdy shakes his hand, offering no reply.

"I said I wasn't stealing your laptop. If I was, would I have stayed here at the table, just holding it up into the air?"

Rialdy shrugs. "Look, you didn't take the laptop, let's leave it at that."

"All right. I need to get the second half of the show started anyhow."

Rialdy watches as Fimandi moves calmly back to the stage and announces, "Second portion of the evening starts now!" He holds up his hands as the crowd applauds.

Eva walks in, sees Rialdy, waves and comes to sit with him. The man who asked him if he were someone's boyfriend nods smugly and points a finger at Rialdy, as though to say 'That's the kind of man you are, you're someone's boyfriend and yet you deny it.'

He doesn't know how to greet Eva. "So?" he says. "Got off

work?"

It feels like the kind of thing a boyfriend would say.

Fimandi calls out to Eva. "I can see Eva sitting over there. Eva, do you want to come up?"

Eva walks toward the stage with a mannered swaying of her hips. Rialdy notes that she receives a fair amount of applause just for doing so.

She plugs a portable device into a console to the side of the stage. A few moments later the bar fills up with the sound of two violin melodies chasing one another, then a measured tambourine, then Eva begins to sing. Rialdy can't quite make out the lyrics because it's sung in a regional Aranacian accent that's unintelligible to him. The song is well-known: many people in the bar join in, though Eva's voice towers over theirs by sheer volume. Apparently it's a funny song. The audience breaks out in laughter at appropriate moments between verses.

Rialdy notices how she changed before coming. In lieu of her austere receptionist clothes, she's wearing a black evening dress that hugs her form.

The end of the song is drowned in raucous applause. Eva stands there beaming, basking in the attention with undisguised pleasure. She stands and waves to people. It becomes manifest that she won't leave the stage without some instigation, so Fimandi approaches and gently places a hand on her back. Still doesn't move. He gives her a little shove. Her eyes go wide in surprise, then she heads back to the Rialdy's table, head swiveling now and then to catch straying audience stares.

"That was really nice," says Rialdy. "You have a lot of talent."

"Do I?" Her eyes betray some distant hurt.

"Definitely. I'd listen to that all day."

"If you listen to a song too much, you don't hear it anymore."

"I know. It's just a figure of speech. I could listen to it a lot."

"Just listening to it a lot, though."

"I know, I know. Your brain starts to predict what's coming, then the element of surprise disappears, then you stop to feel moved by it. We are moved only so long as we are unfamiliar enough with the object that we retain a curiosity for it, while at the same time it has to evoke something inherently familiar, linked to one's personal story."

He feels clever having said that, but she's looking away, not listening. Around them, people frown and hold fingers to lips, "shhh", because by now someone else is on stage reciting a poem in a very low voice, so shy that he holds his page in trembling hands, close enough to his face to hide behind it. Rialdy watches the poet drone on, stealing glances at Eva's arms and neckline. Her arms are chiseled and firm. She holds her head high, chin up. She looks capable, like someone who makes decisions and sticks to them.

Fimandi announces the end of the evening. As they get up, the man at the table next to them who'd called him a boyfriend is still throwing him smug looks, exaggerating his head movement as he nods. Rialdy throws a hand up, palm facing upward, as though to say 'What can I say? You seem to know me better than I know myself.'

Outside, Rialdy and Eva face one another.

"Enjoy your evening?" asks Eva.

"I did! It was a lot of fun. Took my mind off encryption."

The man who'd called him a boyfriend is standing not far from him, smoking a cigarette. "Is that what you do? Encryption?"

Rialdy glowers at him. "Yes, that is what I do for work."

"So," the man says, "you are good with secrets." He arches his eyebrows knowingly toward Eva.

"It's just a job," snaps Rialdy. He turns to Eva. "What's that guy's problem, anyway?"

"Oh, you know," laughs Eva. "He doesn't have a life. If he did he wouldn't be coming here."

"He's indiscreet. But I guess I should relax. The host, what's his name?"

"Fimandi."

"Yeah, Fimandi was just checking out my laptop and, well, I didn't accuse him of trying to steal it, but I didn't deny it when he asked me if I was accusing him. Maybe that guy's right, maybe working in encryption and security does change the way you interact with people, undoing the basic trust in people have that makes them human, approachable …"

"Fimandi was definitely trying to steal your laptop. He steals things all the time. He doesn't feel guilty about it because as a host he isn't paid. The bar just provides him with free drinks. He helps himself to people's things."

"Really? People know about it?"

"It's late. You should be getting back to your hotel."

Rialdy gazes around sheepishly. "I'm not sure I can still find it. I've had a lot to drink."

Eva laughs. "Do you want me to drive you back?"

"Would you mind?"

9

Max sits in his van facing the café, sipping a coffee from a polystyrene cup. Now and then he looks at his watch. Tascha orders her coffee here every morning around 10.

She walks in with Frin at 9:55, holding his hand. she seems to be leading, Frin indulging her. Max watches as they move to the counter, queue, order coffee and get a table. He pushes opens the door of his van and slides off the seat, hitting the pavement with a jolt, still holding his polystyrene coffee cup. Slamming the door of the van behind him, he crosses the street, strides into the café, walks up to Tascha and Frin's table and sits down. With his sunglasses, his unwashed clothes and his new haircut, they don't at first recognize him.

"How are you lovebirds doing?" asks Max.

Tascha is about to respond when one of the café employees comes to stand at their table. "I'm sorry sir, you can't bring your own beverage into the café."

Max holds up a hand but doesn't turn to look at the employee. "I'll only be a moment."

The employee insists, "I have to ask you to either throw your beverage in the bin or leave the premises."

"I said I'll only be a moment."

"Sir, if you're not a paying customer, then I have to ask you to leave the premises."

Max turns to him, annoyed at him for spoiling the surprise, for giving Tascha and Frin time to assess and adjust. He stands up close to the employee and brushes up against him, thinking to push him back, but the employee doesn't budge and the brushing becomes awkward. He chucks his polystyrene cup into the garbage bin and queues to get another. At their table, Tascha and Frin glance at him from an oblique angle, speaking in hushed voices. Max, facing backward in the queue to look at them, moves a step backward every time the queue moves a step forward. He takes the step deliberately, smoothly, as though he can sense how the line is moving. In reality, he's getting that information from the reflection on the inside of his sunglasses lens.

He gets a large coffee with soy milk and no intention of finishing it, just to announce to Tascha and Frin that he's prepared to stay for some time. He sits at their table, pops the plastic cap off the cup, opens three paper sugar packets and pours them in slowly, letting the crystallized sugar cascade and reflect in his sunglasses. He then fixes the plastic cap back on the coffee cup and takes a big, noisy slurp from the cap's small rectangular opening.

Tascha and Frin wait patiently for him to speak first.

"So," says Max. "I missed you leaving after the orgy. Did you intend to come back, or were you just going to ignore my texts forever?"

Tascha starts, "Max —"

"What orgy?" inquires Frin.

"— By the way," pursues Max, "I found you because you've been coming to this same café every day and paying with your bank card, which registers on the online statements. So if you wanted to disappear mysteriously, you did a poor fucking job of it."

"I didn't want to disappear," says Tascha. "I wanted the opposite of that. I wanted to appear. Be visible in my own life. Truly exist."

Max turns to Frin. "Are you the one who's putting this bullshit into her head?"

"Max," says Frin.

Max waits. It embarrasses Frin, who expected an interruption. He really doesn't know what to say apart from 'Max.'

Frin shifts uncomfortably, turns to Tascha. "Would you like me to leave you alone?"

"Stay," says Tascha. "You're in this with me, with us."

"Do you mean us," says Max, "like, you and I, or do you mean us like you, me, and this fucker here? Because that is just gross."

"Max, I came here to meet Doctor Tescar," says Tascha. "He works at the university not far from away. I wanted to ask him about my moods and my weird erratic behavior. I came with Frin because in some way that I don't understand, and that he doesn't either, our souls have bonded, and whatever is happening to me he's a part of. Frin stole the tank from the army base. And he's done some weird things since then."

"Like what?"

"Max," says Frin.

This time he's sure that Max will interrupt him but once again Max just turns to him and waits. Frin gives an embarrassed sigh, purses his lips. With a soulful gaze he signifies that he's with Max, as though they were still in the Extrapolist church, everyone being with everyone, though he's since left the church over ideological differences.

Max sighs too, tired of making Frin uncomfortable. "I went to see Doctor Tescar yesterday too. He told me that the whole coupling program only worked that first year, and that it only existed because there were xenophobic political forces that wanted us refugees cleansed of our original cultures."

Tascha slaps the table. "There! You see? We have entire pans of our existence that have been blanketed. My psyche wants to know, Max! That's what my body is expressing through the craziness. And it's affecting you too! What's with the weird haircut? It could be a vestigial expression of the world we came from."

"It just looks cool," replies Max, dejected.

"Cool," echoes Tascha. "'Cool' means more than 'cool', it's an expression of something lurking under the surface, invisible to us but deeply felt. We say 'cool' but we are evoking worlds, ocean depths and forgotten past lives."

Max strokes his hair self-consciously. He turns to Frin. "Frin, take a walk, will you? I want to speak to Tascha alone."

"We're all in this together, Max. You, Tascha, me..."

Tascha pats his hand. "Take a walk, Frin."

Max grins at Frin. Frin returns a look of strained and annoyed compassion, gets up, exits the café.

Max waits for Frin to leave, continuing to stare at his figure through the large café window as he disappears around the corner. He turns to Tascha. "Time to come home, Tasch. This has lasted long enough. You believe that our souls are linked. Well if they are, we can't be living apart. You know, whatever dream was created years ago in the institute, that we've been dreaming together, may be over. But then, maybe waking up from it is the only way we'll become adults now. From here on we won't be carried by a prefabricated dream. We'll build our own dream, you and me. Let's have our new beginning. Let's have the beginning that we should have had originally. An organic one, that grows out of its own design —"

"I can't even see your eyes when you're talking," says Tascha. "Take off your sunglasses."

Max removes his sunglasses and casually chucks them onto the table. "I forgot I had them on."

Tascha stares at him intensely for a few moments. Max opens his mouth to talk but she cuts him off. "No, don't say anything." He remains there, meeting her gaze, waiting for whatever assessment she's preparing to deliver. Finally she says, "I don't think we ever did that, really truly looked at each other."

Frin is already back peering in at them through the café window.

"Come home, Tascha."

Tascha shakes her head. "I need to stay here for the time being. I still want answers from Doctor Tescar."

"Didn't you talk to him? He told me you went to see him."

Tascha laughs, a full-throated laugh, buttressed with a strange energy that Max finds unsettling. "I asked him, yes, and he gave a few answers. But he gave me the answers that he wanted to give me. He didn't give me the answers that I wanted from him. He will, though."

"Forget it, Tascha. Just come home."

"Where is home, Max? My home is my memories. I have to find them again. Frin was infected by whatever they were, in a way you never were in 15 years of living together. I'm not blaming you. But it means more to me than your notion of some dream. We don't catch colds from other species."

Max looks at Frin in annoyance and brusquely gestures for him to move away from the window. Frin, hands cupped on the window to block out the surrounding light, doesn't budge.

"What do I have to do, Tascha, to convince you? Do I have to steal a tank from a military base? Do I have to do something spontaneous and stupid? Is that what gets you wet?"

"You wouldn't believe." Tascha says it in a dead voice and a stare that looks as though a mask in her likeness has descended on her face. Max is now sitting in front of a stranger. He puts his sunglasses back on. "Our memories are gone, Tascha. Why don't you try to live in the world where you are instead of looking for some hypothetical home?"

"We all have to go home, Max. You have to go home too. After you get up, when you leave this café, you'll tell yourself, 'Hey, I need to go home now.' Where will you go, Max?"

"I'll go home, you fucking moron." Max stands up. "Frin can have you. I don't want you anymore."

Tascha scoffs. "You still want me. Don't lie to yourself."

"Stop believing dumb shit, Tascha. Stop thinking you're smart because you believe things that sound smart but are just baseless analogies and empty words." He walks toward the exit, carrying his oversize coffee, slurping from it as he walks.

Tascha calls out after him, "Go home, Max!"

He turns one last time before leaving the café. "I am going home! I even have a beverage for the ride home." He holds up the coffee and steps through the door, walking backwards.

Outside, he transfers the coffee from his right to his left hand, walks up to Frin and tries to punch him. Frin moves backwards with surprising agility and Max ends up swinging into empty air. He straightens up and takes another slurp of his coffee.

"You can have Tascha," he announces. "I don't want her anymore."

Frin nods. "Thank you, Max. This means more to me than you know." He holds out his arms for a conciliatory hug. Max tries to punch him again and once again fails as Frin jumps backward. He turns and walks to his van, throwing the coffee into the street and watching it bounce, then roll.

He climbs up into his van. Through the window he sees Frin standing by the café, motionless. He pulls down the window of the van.

"Hey Frin, why don't you go pick up that coffee I just dumped? It's still drinkable, there's a top on it. Go pick it up, Frin."

Frin stands there silently.

"Go pick it up, it's right there. Isn't that what you do? Pick up the things I don't want anymore? Eh, Frin?"

Frin shakes his head.

"Go pick up my garbage, Frin. It's half drunk. The cream is all gone, it's just plain coffee, but that shouldn't stop you, you like the things I don't want anymore."

He waits a few moments, glaring at him, then shakes his head, starts the van, and drives off. He sees Frin in his rearview mirror waving at him, a weary, slow wave that looks genuinely heartfelt. He accelerates and drives straight to the city gate, spots the exit that leads to the mountains, and turns into it. Tascha's evocation of home stings as it repeats itself incessantly in his head. 'Home. Home. Home.' He stops the van, turns it around, and heads back.

...

Tascha and Frin are leaving the café, walking along the

sidewalk. Max stops the van beside them and leans out the window. "Hey!"

They stop. "What is it?" asks Tascha with a knowing smirk, as though she knows what's coming next.

"What's the name of the town where the institute was? I can't remember it."

"You're going back there?"

"Just tell me."

"What are you going there for?"

"What's the name of the town?"

Tascha pauses, crossing her arms, nibbling on the inside of her mouth. "Why can't you remember?"

"I don't know! It was so long ago. What does it matter?"

Tascha looks away, then back at him. "It's Terrytown. The town of Terry. We never knew who Terry was. Don't you remember the running gag about looking for Terry?"

"Terrytown," repeats Max. The name is instantly familiar to him and he wonders at how it could have slipped his mind when Doctor Tescar told it to him the previous day. "OK, then. Fuck you both, by the way."

He accelerates a few meters, brakes. He leans out the window even further, twisting his torso toward them. "Hey! Where is Terrytown anyway?"

"South."

"Thanks. Fuck you."

He revs the van and speeds off, not looking in his rear view mirror this time.

...

A few kilometers outside of Terrytown he begins to see the signs for the Terrytown zoo. The signs are old, paint peeling and set alongside the highway signs, mounted on rotting wooden poles. There are painted elephants and ostriches, and it seemed as though there are some crucial animal missing, though the zoo should logically harbor dozens of different species and there's no particular reason to include any one species instead of another, except that some are a bigger draw than others.

He reaches the limits of Terrytown. The landscapes are

suddenly familiar to him. He drives past the convenience stores, the post office, the hardware store. Memories flood over him. Tascha and him getting an ice cream in the middle of summer with money he'd been earning working at a lumber yard while in the semi-detached phase of the institute program. Institute couples trying and failing to get into a local bar. Morning runs on the main street. His eyes fill with tears. He wishes they were all here with him to experience this: Tascha, Gimel, Taltra, Baran, Sinvia. Why haven't any of them ever come back here?

He reaches the institute. The building has been converted into a senior citizen's residence. Next to the institute however, the zoo is still open. He parks in the largely deserted parking lot and gets out of the van, stretching his legs.

He feels rather than hears a sound of breathing, as though someone were standing very close to him. He turns around, then around again, seeing no one. Puzzled, he stops to focus on the sound. Though he can find no source to it, and it seems as though it were originating from directly inside his head.

He buys a ticket at the entrance and walks in. The breathing sound disappears, replaced by the occasional grunt, somewhere between amused and curious. He walks around the zoo, gazing at the listless animals sleeping in the sun in their enclosures, walking lazily along the fences, chewing food scooped from dispensers.

Around a bend he comes upon a fake mountain made of synthetic rubber.

The grunts inside his head stop. He hears a distinct voice, struggling with pronunciation as though it hasn't spoken in a long time. "You're here. You're finally here. Come closer. Get me out here."

10

Eva's house is small and tastefully decorated. Much of the furniture is made of wood and gives the place an overall nature vibe. Rialdy didn't see the signs, the night before as they groped at each other in the entrance, on the staircase, in the bedroom, that she doesn't live alone, that she shares this bedroom with a husband. He notices it now as he wakes up: the male wardrobe, the men's shoes in the corner, the table next to the bed piled with odd electronics parts.

"You didn't tell me you were married."

"My husband is on a business trip," explains Eva, sitting up in bed. "Like you."

"Oh," says Rialdy. "What does he do?"

"He's a researcher."

"Wow, smart guy." Rialdy gets up and goes over to the window. It gives directly onto a forest. They are just a few kilometers outside of the city but already it's wilderness.

"I'm a smart girl too. I was a researcher. That's how we met."

Rialdy arches his eyebrows, but doesn't ask how she went from being a researcher to being a receptionist. New lovers don't react well to perceived judgment.

Eva's side of the bed faces a library crammed with books top to bottom, all of the same design and color scheme as the one she'd been reading at work. He scans it up and down.

"More gods stories?"

Eva nods. "The gods stories are how Aranacians used to explain the way the universe works."

She pauses, as though unsure whether to continue. Having decided, her voice grows animated.

"The gods are not what you would think they are. They aren't characters with superhuman abilities outside of the realm of men but interfering. They were the scientific principles of the time, to which people gave names. They were entropy, and the life cycles. They were the embodiment of people's worldview, the way people chose to remember them. Knowledge, the kind you can't just sum up but have to illustrate symbolically, was imparted through these stories, so characters were required, otherwise people would give up trying to keep them in mind. This," she gestures toward her shelf of books, "is the entire science library of a past civilization."

Rialdy hears a cough somewhere and is surprised at how it fails to alarm him.

"I can see the interest in old science," said Rialdy. "Science science can be pretty dry."

"I studied science. I was surrounded by rational people, engineers and mathematicians and others who can take a model and apply it directly to existence. But it comes at a price, where the psyche is concerned. It prevents you from allowing yourself to be submerged by the richness of the day to day. It prevents you from seeing the gods."

Rialdy briefly wonders what kind of problems are awaiting him with Eva. He hears the cough again.

"Does someone else live here?"

"My husband isn't here, if that's what you're asking. He's traveling for his work. Would you like some breakfast?"

They dance around the bed picking up their respective clothes, avoiding each other's bodies. Rialdy jumps up to pull his pant legs over his feet, jolting himself into full wakefulness. They head downstairs to the kitchen. Rialdy sees at the four chairs surrounding the kitchen table and wonders which one is Eva's husband's. He hears a snicker from somewhere and turns to see where it came from but can't quite place it.

Eva stands at the stove, smiling. "Please," she says. "Sit down! You're not in a rush to get to work, are you? You've been staying late at work for some time now, I'm sure you can take some morning time for yourself."

Rialdy sits down uneasily. A small monkey hops into the kitchen on webbed feet. It has a pink face and small eyes that dart around nervously as it hops.

"Hello, Magic Man," greets Eva. She kneels and puts out her hands to welcome the monkey, who hops toward her and jumps lightly into her arms, pulls and scratches his way onto her shoulder and turns to wrap long, spindly arms around her face, covering her nose, gripping onto her untied hair. Eva laughs and stands up. The monkey withdraws its arms from around her head and eyes Rialdy, yawning and licking his hands.

"That is one cool monkey!" exclaims Rialdy.

"You can hear me. You can hear my voice." He could have sworn that the voice just came from the monkey, but the monkey hasn't opened its mouth and no sound has emanated from him. Rialdy blinks a few times.

"Does he...talk?"

Eva laughs. "Of course not! he's a monkey, not a parrot!" She turns her head and puckers her lips, asking for a kiss. The monkey turns and dutifully touches his mouth to hers. "His name is Gimmee," explains Eva. "I gave him that name. The day I got him, I just looked at him for some time and I decided that he looked like a Gimmee."

"That's actually my name," says the monkey's voice.

"Your monkey is talking to me," says Rialdy.

Eva looks at him with a puzzled frown, as though she's not sure whether or not he's being serious, but there's also a flicker of recognition in her face. "Maybe you have a privileged relationship with animals of all kinds?"

Gimmee's gaze continues to dart around nervously, in opposition to the easy, familiar tone that Rialdy is perceiving. He can't determine if the voice is actual sound or if it's resonating purely within his own mind. It's like trying to identify the color of a wall seen in pre-dawn semi-darkness.

"It was the one and only time she picked up on my voice," says Gimmee. "I thought she might be a proper receptor, but she lacks a whole level of sensitivity. That's probably what makes her such a lousy musician."

Rialdy stares at the monkey, debating whether to address him directly in front of Eva.

"OK," says Eva. "Let's get some food in your belly. You must be hungry."

Rialdy sighs and nods. The monkey hops off Eva's shoulder onto the counter and along it.

"How old is your monkey?" asks Rialdy.

Eva sets a plate in front of him and begins to lay down the breakfast staples: butter, sugar, milk for coffee, smoke flavor. "I've had him for, oh, five years maybe? He was left to me by a friend."

Rialdy nods. "Is he native to Aranacia?"

"Do you think any primate except man would strive in this freezing environment?" asks Gimmee. "I was brought over here. If I'm being honest, I've lived here too long, too. You're a particularly good receptor. You don't play music though. That's a shame. You might've been talented. You'll probably die without ever knowing what potential you had. But that's what existence is, a lot of unexplored possibilities. Did you enjoy fucking Eva? She's married, you know."

At this point the monkey's nose twitches in a rapid vibratory movement. Gimmee's voice emits something like a snort. Again, Rialdy struggles to determine if the snort is a physical sound or some kind of understanding he has that the monkey just communicated a sarcastic grunt.

Weirded out, he suddenly stands up. "You know what? I should go. I need to get back to the hotel before heading to work. I have some documents I need to work on today." He heads toward the house entrance. Eva follows.

"Wait, how will you get there? The bus doesn't come by for another hour. If you just wait, I can drive you."

Rialdy stops at the front door. The monkey is snorting openly now, guffawing. Unmistakably, he's making actual sounds, clapping together his minute hands with their long, slender, clawed fingers. Screeching. It occurs to Rialdy, alongside the disembodied chuckles, that whatever he heard of the monkey's voice, it's not a physical one.

He turns to glare, through the living room, through the narrow corridor, all the way to the kitchen counter, directly at the laughing monkey.

Eva runs to Gimmee. "It's OK, baby," she says. She turns to Rialdy. "He gets upset at sudden movements and loud voices. He's very sensitive."

"Sensitive!" says Gimmee's voice. "Me! I wish!"

Rialdy heads reluctantly back to the kitchen. The monkey waits for him with placidly bowed shoulders. Rialdy leans toward him and stares at him fixedly. "What are you?"

Eva looks from Rialdy to the monkey. The monkey screeches and claps his hands together, emitting no sound.

"Come on!" laughs Eva. "Sit down and have breakfast with me! What's the problem? I'm not asking anything of you, Rialdy. Just have breakfast, let me do that for you. Being a good host is a big part of the Aranacian psychology. We like to receive."

"And how she receives," adds Gimmee.

Rialdy sits. He eats four slices of toast with butter and jam, drinks two coffees with milk and sugar. All the while, he's acutely aware, through his peripheral vision, of the monkey sitting on the counter, chattering ceaselessly in a rambling monologue.

"You don't know how rare it is to find a receptor. You're the first one I've met in years. I certainly didn't expect Eva to bring one home, though I will admit that every time her husband goes on a trip and she goes to that bring-your-own-culture event, a little hope is kindled in me that she will. You have an interesting mind, Rialdy. Not interesting in the sense of experiences, more like interesting in the way desert sand can be beautiful when seen from very far away because it starts to look like a sea. Your mind is like that, boring and flat, but it does tend to reflect your environment like a mirror, which is probably why you're a good receptor."

Rialdy chews his breakfast in sullen silence, seething at the monkey's abuse. Gimmee stops at times, seeming to momentarily regret the harshness of his words, then after a pause he resumes again, as though it were beyond his ability to stop himself anyhow. Rialdy looks up now and then from his food to glare at him. Eva mistakes his glare for interest.

"Gimmee is very intelligent," she says. "It's surprising how intelligent he is, given the small size of his cranium. You know, some days I'm convinced he understands everything I say, absolutely everything."

Rialdy finishes his plate, downs his coffee in one big gulp. He pushes away from the table, crosses his arms and waits for her to finish.

The monkey keeps talking.

"I can see from your mind that your girlfriend and you are trying to conceive. So I guess what this is is practice, eh? If at first you don't succeed then try again, and again, and again. With other people. That seems to be your pattern, just going with whatever feeling you happen to be in at any moment. Totally at odds with a plan to conceive, or planning anything. If you would just inspect that plan, you'd see how irresponsible it is. How do you compare Tace and Eva's bodies? It's complicated, isn't it? Tace may be softer, more cushioned, but Eva is strong, and you realize you like a woman with a little muscle on her, like she could punch you out if she wanted to. You'd like that. You'd like to be physically punished. You enjoyed gripping that muscle, her thighs especially, just gripping and not letting go. Why grip thighs? What's the point? Maybe it has to do with testing a potential mate's running capacity? Who knows?"

Rialdy grits his teeth. Eva leisurely finishes eating, then wipes her mouth. She's noted Rialdy's agitation and it puzzles her. She clears her throat. "I'll just take a shower, then I can drive you back to your hotel."

"Actually, we may as well just go straight to work."

"You said you needed your documents?"

"Come to think of it, I can do without them."

She nods. "OK. I won't be long. I'm not working until later so it's just the shower, no work preparation. No makeup." She touches her face.

Eva clears the table, piles the dishes in the sink, then leaves them alone in the kitchen. Rialdy waits as he hears her climb the staircase, traverse a corridor, enter the bathroom and shut the door before he turns once more to the monkey.

"What are you? How are you doing this?"

"I'm a river monkey," says Gimmee, his mouth obstinately closed. "There are very few of us left. We could have ruled the world, through you humans. But too many of us got sick. The remaining ones, like myself, are those that don't have the muscle. So I sit here, in Eva's house, bored and angry all the time. It's nice to have someone to talk to, but then I don't see you as buddy material. You don't have the ability to relax."

"River monkey," repeats Rialdy, out loud. "Where are the river monkeys from?"

"We came from far East. Our island was somewhere south of Indonesia. When the men first came we couldn't speak to them the way we spoke among ourselves, through the mind. Otherwise we'd just have told them to leave. We could have made them leave."

The monkey marks a pause.

"Listen, Rialdy. I need to get back home. I can't die here in Aranacia all alone. I need to be with others of my own kind, do you understand? None of us really exist when we're separate. This power that you're experiencing, the mind to mind communication, it's nothing in comparison to our real capacities. When the river monkeys come together, as a society, our minds meld into one super-mind, and the thoughts of this super-mind are beautiful beyond anything that you've ever known, believe me."

"Why would I —" Rialdy realizes his voice is loud enough to be heard from upstairs and brings it down to a whisper. "Why would I help you, you fucking bitter monkey?" His whisper sounds like a hiss.

"You know," the monkey's voice hisses back, hisses even in the disembodied way it comes to him, from somewhere inside his own head that strangely feels as though it was outside his head, but not outside around his body, "you don't have to use your mouth to talk to me. If you just narrate the voice in your head like you're in a movie, I'll hear it and Eva won't have to know you're yelling at her companion and pet." He pauses. "Really, man, listen to yourself. You're hissing at a monkey you just met."

"Look, I have my life, my plans, I can't take vacation time to accompany some monkey on a home trip. You look alright here. Eva likes you. You probably eat all you like. Let's just —"

"I can show you your mother's grave."

II

He should be surprised to hear a disembodied voice in a zoo, but no. Max approaches the fence and leans against it, aware of the voice, in no hurry to identify the source. He scans the rubber-clad hill left to right, taking in the strange surface, the fake polystyrene haphazardly-placed rocks, resembling the moon's surface.

Max mentally projects his voice. "What are they going for here? Moon landing or volcano?"

He hears a warm, indulgent giggle in reply. It's familiar and the voice comes off as a distant, vague, fond memory.

"I don't know," says the voice. "I've wondered about it for years. Come on, get me out of here."

"Get who out of where? I don't even know who or what you are. Help me out."

"You know what I am. Look up, right near the entrance of the cave. I'm waving to you."

Max sees her then, standing in front of the cave, her fur so close to the cave's color that he initially thought she was just another rock. The monkey is, indeed, waving to him.

"You're a monkey!" exclaims Max, astonished.

"I'm an old friend. You don't remember me, but then that's how it was always supposed to be. You look good, Max. My eyesight isn't what it used to be, though. Don't move, I'll come closer."

The monkey leans forward, dropping her hands to the ground, and hops toward him. It's an ungainly hop, lopsided and awkward, and it's apparent that the monkey has some kind of hip problem. She hops anyway, bearing down the hill toward the tall metal fence at a surprising speed. She reaches the fence and grasps it with her fingers.

Max hunkers down on his knees and places his hands

over the monkey's. The monkey's hands are damp from the ground. Her fingers are bony and trembling.

Aloud, Max asks, "How do I know you?"

The monkey's voice comes to him from inside his own mind. "I'll say my name, and it'll unlock the memory like a key unlocks a door. I should warn you, Max, that once the door is open, a lot of memories will come out, all at the same time, and a lot of them will be rather unpleasant. The unpleasant will probably even outweigh the pleasant, but it can't be helped. I need your help, Max, and I'm sorry I had to get you away from your life to do so, but it can't be helped. So tell me, are you ready?"

Max grasps the monkey's fingers more tightly through the metal fence, lifting them slightly and placing his thumbs under the palms, as though to help her stand up, though the monkey is already standing at full height and barely makes it past Max's knees. Her fur is brown streaked with black, a grey halo around the face in two different shades, one natural, the other showing her age. Her eyes are a deep green, serene and detached, but also holding some sadness. Her eyebrows are bushy and sprout in all directions, evoking infinite possibilities but also worlds destined to remain unexplored, reinforcing the sadness in her eyes. The monkey's tail wags gently back and forth, little movements that evoke either breathing or intrusive thoughts to which she gives no importance.

"There's no going back, right?" asks Max. "If you tell me your name? There'll be no closing that door once it's open?"

The monkey twitches her nose. "I'm sorry, Max. This is going to hurt. Take your time. Be sure."

"I don't know, fuck it, go ahead, tell me your name."

"Warin."

At first there's nothing, just Max holding the monkey's hands through the holes in the metal fence, feeling their slight tremble, seeing the monkey's nose twitch intermittently. There's a slight breeze blowing from the left and Max is aware of the sun's heat. Then, suddenly, he feels it: a horrific sense of loss, of parents disappeared, of a home ripped away. He lets the monkey's fingers slip away from his and sits down brusquely, feeling heavier than he ever remembers feeling before. He opens his mouth to ask 'why' but no sound comes out, just a thin wail. He can't close his mouth or swallow, he can only wail for lost worlds. He drools from his open mouth.

"I'm sorry, Max. Maybe we should have waited."

Max wails, rocks back and forth like a baby. His head strikes against the fence it's soothing enough that he begins to bang it with his forehead again and again. Harder and harder. His sunglasses come off and bounce between the bridge of his nose and the fence before tumbling to the ground as he continues to bang his forehead. He reaches up with his fists and bangs his temples, too. Names pop into his head: his mother's, his father's, sister's, friends'. He hasn't thought of them for years, and now they're present again but also gone, opening huge holes within him and threatening to collapse his core sense of self.

He flops onto his back. His whole body twists and turns over on the gravel pathway in front of the monkey's enclosure. He pummels his temples with his fists, pummels his closed eyes, pummels his cheeks.

He can still hear Warin's voice, soft and apologetic but not soothing. "I'm sorry, Max. It may be painful right now but it's not all bad. And there are other doors I can open for you that will lead to nicer places. It's not all bad, Max. This is the worst of it. From here on, you'll see, it gets better."

Max, writhing on the ground, shakes his head violently.

"Max", says Warin, "I know how painful this is right now. I also need you to get me out of here. There must be a way to cut a hole in this fence, I'm sure you could find some tools in one of the maintenance sheds. You'd just have to cut through a few links, Max. Max?"

Max writhes and wails.

"Come on, Max. Snap out of it. Look, this was a bad idea. We should have waited until later. But then, you had to know exactly why I need to get out of this enclosure. You can sense it, Max, it's right there under your memories. If you can just access it, you'll understand that you have to get me out of here. Max?"

Max's wail grows thinner and turns into a sob.

A caretaker walks up to Max's writhing form. "Are you OK, sir? Did you injure yourself on the fence?"

Warin looks away. Max stops thrashing, feeling silly. He keeps his palms pressed over his eyes and remains on his back. "I just remembered something."

The caretaker clears his throat and moves closer. "Excuse me? Did you say you just remembered something?"

Max sits up, looking up at the caretaker, frightened. "Where do I go now? I have nowhere to go. I have nowhere to go. There's no home anywhere."

The caretaker frowns and squints. "Were you trying to get into the river monkey's enclosure? You know you can't do that."

Max shakes his head. He senses that, if he were to focus intensely on the present instant, he could ignore the flood of memories, which now feel like they've filled some pool and are waiting to be perused and analyzed, one at a time. He stands up. "I wasn't trying to get into any enclosure."

"You can't stay in the zoo. You can't be rolling around in the dirt, either. This is a family place. Children come here."

"What?"

"It's a question of propriety."

The caretaker turns to stare at Warin. "What is it with you, Peaches? People are always getting weird around you."

Warin stares up at the caretaker. She looks contrite. Her nose twitches thoughtfully.

Max turns and staggers off along the path from which he came. The caretaker follows him, running a few steps to catch up. "It's not really my job to tell people this, but I'd rather you heard it from me than from the guys in charge of zoo security." Max nods. His eyes are filling with tears again, welling up from a place he didn't know he had. The caretaker settles into Max's walking pace, remaining by his side. "Those guys take their job to heart. They can be verbally abusive, and they can get pretty physical, too. Rules and force."

Max nods. He doesn't trust his voice to speak.

"Are you leaving the zoo?" asks the caretaker. "Are you on your way out?"

Max nods again. "I don't know where I'm going, though. This was the last place I could think of going to, and now I have to leave, so I don't know where I'm going."

"Don't you have some home you can go to?"

"Everyone uses that word," says Max. "Everyone talks of home." He shakes his head. "Look, thanks for saving me from the security guys, but you know, I could take both of them. I know how to fight."

The caretaker nods and sticks out a hand. "My name's Jine. I work with the primates and the rodents that look sort of like primates."

Max waves away the hand. "I really don't care who you are."

"Hey," says Jine. "You said you don't have anywhere to go, right? That you don't have a home?"

Max shrugs. "I'll survive. I've come this far. I'm not dead yet."

"Well, why don't you have some ice cream before you go? It's on me. Just come over to the food section and sit down a while, have some ice cream. It might help you see things in a whole new light."

Max stops walking and echoes, "ice cream."

"Come on, who doesn't like ice cream? Just come sit down a few minutes. What do you have to lose?"

"OK," says Max. "I'll have some ice cream."

...

They sit at a large outdoor picnic table, each man holding a large ice cream cone carrying three balls of different-flavored ice cream. Jine has chosen coffee, exotic fruit and chocolate. Max has chosen sweet cheese, nuts and coffee. Jine offered to pay for Max's ice cream but Max declined, saying he didn't lack for money.

Max licks the ice cream absent-mindedly, though

inwardly he's observing his pain and trying not to mentally move too much. Any memory he accesses triggers its own aching stab. Jine discreetly observes Max, staring at the cages of the large cats, then occasionally darting a glance back at Max.

"Hey," says Jine, "tell me Max, what's your favorite animal at the zoo?"

Max shrugs. "Elephants."

"We don't have elephants here."

"Do you have tigers?"

"No."

"Wolves?"

"We have one mountain wolf."

"Wolves then."

Jine nods and licks his ice cream a few times.

"The thing is, you were having your lie-down session in front of Peaches' enclosure. I mean, you chose that enclosure to let whatever personal crisis you were in come to the surface."

"Yeah, so?"

Jine leans forward a little. "The thing is, you see, when weird things happen around here, they usually happen around Peaches' enclosure. It's like people pick that spot to have their meltdowns."

Max stops licking his ice cream a moment, then resumes. "Does it happen a lot?"

"It happens. I've been working here for more than ten years, and nothing else I ever saw was as weird as the things that happen in front of that enclosure. I have to ask you, what is it about that monkey? What happened to you in front of that enclosure?"

"None of your fucking business is what happened to me."

Jine nods. "Fair enough."

The two men lock stares. Max expects Jine to be cowed, but he's not.

Jine grins. "Hey, I'll arm-wrestle you. If you lose, you tell me what this monkey is about. I know you know."

Max laughs. "If I win?"

"What would you want?"

"If I win, I take the monkey with me when I leave here."

"I'm just a caretaker here, I don't own the zoo."

"I'm sure you can look the other way and let me do what I need to do."

They finish their ice creams, trading leisurely licks for full bites. Max plants his elbow on the table and opens his hand, wriggling the fingers. Jine puts his own elbow down in front of Max's, rolls his thumb around Max's, shifts his hand around a little, and carefully wraps his fingers around the hand. "You say when."

"Go," says Max. His whole arm flexes, the shoulder tensing along with his neck muscles. He lurches forward and throws all his weight behind his arm. Jine's hand moves down a little. The locked arms tremble. Jine keeps smiling. Max frowns. He focuses his efforts on another push. Jine, still smiling, firms his grip, takes a deep breath, and tugs. The men's gripped hands move up to the apex then crash over on the other side like a falling tree, rapping Max's hand on the wood of the picnic table.

Jine made it look effortless.

"Fuck," says Max, rubbing the knuckles of his hand. "You're stronger than you look."

"The thing about arm wrestling is, it's all about how you set up the grip, initially. If you get a stronger position, you can come out on top, even with people who are stronger than you. In this case, I think I'm stronger than you anyway, but it really is about getting a good grip. I try to apply that in life."

"I'm sure there are many opportunities for a zoo caretaker to apply life strategies."

"So tell me, what's your story, Max? I want to know what it has to do with this monkey."

"Well," says Max, looking thoughtfully away at a row of trees in the distance. "My wife left me. We're not married, but it's like we are. Anyway, that's what made me leave the house. I've been driving, wandering. I saw this zoo and I walked in. There was an enclosure with the monkey. The monkey reminded me of my wife. That's it."

"That's bullshit."

"No, it's not."

"Your wife looks like a knee-high monkey with a furry face and fingers like claws? Why would anyone live with a woman who looks like that?"

"I said the monkey reminded me of her. I didn't say it looked like her. I'd like to believe that I can do better than that. But, none of that matters. I'd have been with her no matter what she looked like."

"Wait, back up though. How did the monkey remind you of your wife?"

"Hey, Jine, thanks for the ice cream break. It was nice meeting you. I might be back soon."

Max stands and made his way to the zoo exit.

12

Rialdy stares at his computer screen. He's been sitting and staring at the same block of code for the last five minutes and can't bring himself to make the necessary changes to it to enclose it in the Empiricole encryption template and move on to the next block. His mind drifts back and forth from block of code to childhood memories. He sighs, gets up, and walks to the door of the small office where he's been working alone for weeks. He leans against the door, peering into the corridor. Most of the faces on his floor are by now familiar to him but he seldom talks to anyone except when greeting them in the morning when they come in and in the evening when he's leaving. He's seen as a punctual presence, passing through, fleeting. Beyond a vague curiosity, the other workers on his floor take little or no interest in him. The top shelf of his office library holds tea and sugar that people walk in all day to help themselves to, rarely looking at him or saying a word as they do so.

He goes to the elevator, veers into the stairwell and pulls out a cigarette. There are non-smoking signs in the stairwell but the ground is littered with butts, attesting to the discrepancy between rules and their enforcement typical of Aranacia. As he smokes, he leans into the center of the stairwell and looks down. There were so many floors that the center retracts into a distant, tiny hole enclosed in a complex geometrical pattern. He can't make out the ground floor. He considers dropping something down, to time its fall to the floor. He decides to check it out for himself.

Snuffing out his cigarette under his work shoe, he kicks it into the pile of butts by the stairwell door, then begins to descend the stairs. The concrete walls, painted a dull blue all the way down to his floor, turn quite bare, covered with a strange soot that renders them a dull brown-orange color. An odor grows stronger, a mix of damp earth, chemicals, and something else besides, sickly sweet. He descends all the way to the bottom floor, expecting the door to be locked. He turns the handle. The door clicks open.

Above the door a strange sign is nailed, depicting a stick man with lines that emanate from his body, ending in question marks. He stares at it a moment, trying to make sense of it, then gives up and pushes open the door to the mine.

The main chamber of the mine. There's another metal staircase that shoots straight down at a lurching angle, at the bottom of which hulks a large machine with multiple screens, buttons, dials, and embedded keyboards. The staircase starts at ceiling level, and as he descends the full chamber comes into view, hundreds of meters across and almost the same in width, forking at one end into five distinct, dimly-lit tunnels.

He reaches the control machine. A man standing in front of it, wearing a mining helmet, turns to face him.

"You have no business here," he says in rough Aranacian. "Why are you here?"

Despite the harshness of his words, the man's tone is amused. Nevertheless afraid he may have gotten himself into trouble, Rialdy tries to make a joke out of it.

"I just wanted to know what that sign outside says. Tell me that and I'll leave."

The man laughs. Rialdy isn't sure he's buying it, but it seems like he won't make trouble.

"Sterility warning. Toxic fumes from the mine. You work here, you don't have babies. That's why there are lines going to the question marks. They should be going to the stick man's children, but he can't have any. So, question marks." He smiles, shrugs and waves Rialdy backward. "You have to leave now."

Rialdy nods and starts to step back. A question occurs to him. "What do you wear to protect against it?"

"Nothing. You only come work in this mine if you've already had children. Cheaper for birth control. Once you work in the mine, no more kids. That's just the way it is. The pay's good here."

"Oh! I should head back up then. I don't want to go sterile."

The man arches his eyebrows. "Have you been working in the building?"

"Yes, but much higher up. I'm only fifty floors below the surface."

"Fifty, thirty, seventy, the fumes and soot don't care. They go where they want. How long have you been working here?"

"It's been a little over a month. I was supposed to be just one month, but —"

The man interrupts him with a whistle. "You should get yourself checked by a doctor. But it's probably too late. You won't have children." He looks genuinely pained for Rialdy. "You look young, too. No one told you?"

"My office is much, much higher up than this," protests Rialdy. He can feel a tingling in the back of his neck. His stomach knots.

"Doesn't matter. They paint the walls to hide the soot, but it's there anyway and then there's the fumes." He shakes his head. "Someone should have told you. Anyway, you can't stay here, you have to go back now."

Rialdy backs up, turns and mounts the stairs, going through the door. As the door closes behind him he looks back again at the sign above it. It strikes him even more strongly now, now that he knows what the question marks mean. Though unsure how much to believe of the rugged mine entrance worker's words, he's trembling.

He walks slowly up the steps to his floor, staying as far as he can from the wall and its brown-orange soot. When he reaches his floor, he stops off at the washroom to wash his hands, over and over. Then his forearms. Then his face.

From his office he calls Miles.

"Miles? Did you know about it? About the sterility risk?"

"What?"

"Just tell me if you knew, Miles. Knowing me, my situation, knowing my efforts to conceive with my girlfriend. Tell me you didn't know. I'm listening, Miles. Tell me you didn't know. I hope you didn't know." His hands won't stop trembling.

"I have no idea what you're talking about."

"The entire plant is fucking toxic! Anywhere you work in this shithole you lose the ability to conceive! The mine is toxic and so is every part of the building above it!"

"Wait, if that's the case, I should find something on the internet. Are you looking too?"

"No, I'm not looking on the internet! They don't provide internet connections in computer rooms where the software needs to be encrypted, Miles!"

"OK, hold on, calm down. Let me check."

There's a pause in the conversation. Rialdy hears nothing but Miles' breathing and intermittent keyboard clacking. The clacking seems to be getting more, not less, frantic.

Miles' voice comes on.

"I think I know the real reason they wanted a foreign company to intervene for their security problem. No one else would enter their facility." Miles remains calm but sounds horrified. "You need to get yourself to a doctor as soon as possible, Rialdy. Like, today. Leave the office and go directly."

Rialdy cradles his head in his hands. "I can't believe this is happening."

"Fuck these guys. I'm going to get you a flight home, Rialdy. We don't need to do business with these people. I'm sure we can find some way to sue them."

Rialdy is surprised and touched by Miles' sudden vehemence. He shakes his head. "I'm going to see a doctor. I've been here over a month. A few days less or more won't change that."

He hangs up, still cradling his head in his hands.

...

Eva sits at the reception desk in the lobby. She watches as

Rialdy bursts out of the elevator and half-runs toward her, lips pressed together hard.

"I need to see Azgeviu," spits Rialdy, slamming his palms down on the reception desk counter. Though he's glowering at her, his voice is weaker than usual.

"What do you need to see him about?" asks Eva, reaching for her telephone.

"Don't call him!" snarls Rialdy. "Just tell me where his office is. I want to talk to him face to face."

Eva hesitates, one hand holding the telephone, hovering in midair.

Rialdy's voice goes quiet once more. "Did you know? Did you know too?"

Eva doesn't reply.

"About the toxicity of the plant," insists Rialdy. "About how it takes away your capacity to conceive."

Eva gently puts down the telephone. "Yes, I know. Everyone knows. It affects men and women, otherwise there'd be only the one or the other sex working here. Didn't you know? Didn't anyone tell you? I supposed it didn't matter to you, if you were here."

She looks embarrassed. "I could have told you... You never revealed much about your life. But, I should have asked."

She writes on a piece of paper, folds it in half and hands it to him.

"What's this?"

The question puzzles her. "Azgeviu's office number. It's on the fifth floor. Aren't you going to kill him?"

"Kill him? No, I'm just... I'm going to tell him —"

"If he brought you here, knowing that he was taking away your capacity to have children, if you don't already have children and if you want them, then it's the same as if he strangled your children himself."

"Oh fuck. I'm going to be sick."

"This man removed your descent, Rialdy. Take the paper. Do what you have to do." She brandishes the paper at him. Her eyes are glowing. Rialdy takes it. "I'm not going to kill him," he mumbles. He walks toward the elevator.

"You can always adopt," calls out Eva. The doors of the elevator close. Rialdy clenches his fists and imagines himself punching Azgeviu's face again and again. His fists seem too frail to him for the task. Azgeviu has a huge head. He could break his hands on that massive skull.

He enters Azgeviu's office with fists clenched anyway. Azgeviu looks up as he comes in. Even though he has good reason to, he finds he can't just assault the man. He wonders what temporary insanity means. What kind of information does he have to receive to really fly into a blind rage?

"You knew? When you brought me here, made me work in this plant, that I'd be affected? That I'd become sterile?"

Azgeviu remains seated. He claps his hands together over the desk, then sits back. "Nothing has been proven," he says. "For all we know, it could just be a statistical anomaly."

Rialdy stands, seething, clenching and unclenching his fists.

"Look," says Azgeviu, "it's true that most people who work here don't have children, but nothing has been proven, and we don't base our work practices on hearsay and conjecture. This is Aranacia."

He holds his hands apart, signifying a conclusion. "We have a contract with Empiricole. We expect you to respect the terms."

"We're going to sue you for this, for endangering my life by bringing me here."

Azgeviu produces a full, rasping laugh and slaps the table. "In an international court? With what evidence? There have been no studies to prove anything, and we intend to keep it that way. If anything, you should sue Empiricole who sent you here without properly researching the risks to your person." His laughter turns into a cough, then the tail end of his laughter. Then he clears his throat.

Rialdy leaves Azgeviu's office, heads back down to the lobby, to Eva's desk.

"So? What did you do?" she asks. She seems relaxed, unworried.

"I killed him. He's dead."

"No." Eva smiles tenderly. "You couldn't."

"I'm pretty sure I could."

"Let's just say I didn't think you would."

"Can I see you tonight? Is your husband still on his trip?"

"He is. Would you like to come to my house for supper? I could make you something traditionally Aranacian."

"Sure, that'd be great. Is your monkey there?"

Eva pulls her head back and protrudes her upper lip, making a type of duck face. "Of course. He's always with me. Are you becoming friends with Gimmee?"

Rialdy looks away. "He's cute. He's a cute monkey. Look, I should go, go see a doctor. Is there a doctor you can recommend, who can check if I can still procreate?"

...

The doctor speaks no English. He asks him directly if he's been working out of the Rare Earths Mining Plant. He chuckles when Rialdy acquiesces. "No one told you?"

Rialdy glares at him. He realizes it might be the most aggressive thing he knows how to do. Everyone in Wizniu seems either completely oblivious to it or recognizes it as a bluff.

"Take off all your clothes and sit on the table."

The metal table looks cold. Totally naked, Rialdy hesitates before its smudged surface. "Aren't you going to put something on it before I sit?"

"It's very clean." The doctor indicates the table with an open hand. "Please." He's leaning forward. He looks like he'll fall forward if Rialdy doesn't sit on the table, so Rialdy does. The surface is as cold as it looks. He can feel his skin shrivel and contract on contact. The doctor sits on a low chair and brings his face threateningly close to Rialdy's privates. He squints at Rialdy's scrotum. "Hmm."

"Can you... See something?" asks Rialdy.

"I like to think that I can. I've seen quite a few of these cases. I recognize the effect of the toxin on both male and female genitalia. I'm not a betting man, but if I was, I'd put good money on you never having children. We will test your blood, urine and of course your semen, but, speaking for myself, I don't need those results."

Rialdy shakes his head. "I can't believe anyone actually works in that plant."

The doctor looks up in surprise. "Are you kidding? People fight to get into it. They pay much better than any other business in the vicinity. But beyond that, a lot of people have their reasons to want to lose the ability to have children, without having to have an intervention that would necessitate their partner's approval."

Rialdy frowns. "That doesn't make sense. They need their partner's approval to work there, don't they?"

"They pay much better. And the sterility toxins are certainly a badly-kept secret, but they're nevertheless a secret. Nothing has been proven, and nothing ever will be. Authorities will never allow anyone to conduct a study on premises."

...

Rialdy takes the bus to Eva's, carrying a bottle of wine. They eat in the dining room. Gimmee stares from a perch on a corner of the table. Rialdy avoids mentally conversing with the monkey while Eva's in the room. Following the main course, Eva clears the table and disappears into the kitchen to prepare desert. "Don't peek!" she admonishes.

Rialdy brusquely stands and run-walks over to the monkey. "You can see into my mind," he projects mentally. "Tell me what I want to know."

"You want to know if you'll ever have children."

"Tell me. You can see things, right? Things that are inside me?"

"Pull down your pants and underwear."

Rialdy undoes his belt, unbuttons his pants, pulls them down along with his underwear. He feels silly facing the monkey with exposed privates. He stands a long moment motionless, expectant. Gimmee stares back at him. Gimmee doesn't appear to be looking at his genitalia.

"And now tell me," says Gimmee finally, "do I look like a doctor to you?"

The monkey snickers loudly. Even in the disembodied voice, the snicker is high-pitched and irritating.

Eva walks in carrying two cups of coffee-colored cream topped with fruit, chilled spoon handles jutting out of them. She stops suddenly before Rialdy standing with his pants and underwear down, facing the impassive, seated monkey.

"I was just exposing myself to your monkey."

He pulls up his underwear and pants.

13

Max calls Tascha from the van. He's sitting on the side of the open sliding door, one foot on the edge, the other one hanging over it, swinging. He's watching the sun rise and sipping a beer.

"Hi, Max."

"Hey, Tascha? Tell me, do you remember that monkey who used to walk around the premises of the Institute?"

Tascha thinks a moment.

"I remember. I had a pet name for him. I forget what it was."

"What if I told you that monkey is what made Doctor Tescar's program work? She's staying at the zoo just next to the old Institute and has been there since the Institute closed. She has mind powers. She can talk to you directly into your mind."

"That is such bullshit, Max." Tascha sounds bored. "Why are you making this up?"

"Tascha, I'm serious."

"A monkey with mental powers. That's what you came up with."

"Look, I was at the zoo —"

"Who told you?"

"Who told me what?"

"You're saying Doctor Tescar's program worked accidentally, that it was all thanks to a monkey. Who told you that?"

"I know it sounds strange —"

"It doesn't sound strange. It sounds like shit you're making up to try to manipulate me."

"Manipulate you? Manipulate you into doing what exactly, Tascha?"

He can hear noises on the other end of the line, difficult to identify. Then, Tascha's voice hissing something. Then a moan and a slap. Breathing. Doctor Tescar's voice.

"Max," pleads Doctor Tescar, "help me."

"Doctor Tescar? What are you doing with Tascha?"

"She's secluded me, Max. Tascha and her crazy boyfriend. I don't know what they're going to do to me. They're going to kill me. Please do something, Max. Please. Talk to them, say something."

Tascha's voice comes back on. "Did you hear him, Max? We grabbed the Doctor. That's how you do it, Max. That's how you get answers. If you have any question you want to ask him, shoot them to us and we'll put them to him. We'll make sure you get a straight answer."

"Tascha, that's —"

"It's what needs to be done. And I'm doing it. For you, for me, for the others."

"Tascha ..."

Max's voice catches in his throat. He looks out over the wheat field and beyond, to the tree-bordered road. The swaying of plants, the occasional car slowly cruising by. It's peaceful. His throat constricts, he presses the phone to his forehead. His shoulders shake. He sobs loudly, like a balloon rupturing.

"Max?"

Max hits himself in the face with the phone a few times. He sobs again, cries out wordlessly.

"Max?"

"It hurts so much, Tascha."

"What hurts?"

"I have the memories back. The monkey gave them to me."

"Oh, Max. What the fuck are you talking about?"

"I have the memories back. The Institute, coming here from Canada. My home. My parents. Everyone who's gone, Tascha. Everyone who'll never come back again. I don't know what to do with these memories. It's like they were frozen and now they're fresh."

"You mean like frozen vegetables that you just took out of the freezer, to thaw them out? The way they're actually fresher than fresh vegetables because they freeze them right after they've being picked?"

"I don't know, Tascha. But yeah, really fresh."

"Max. I'm sorry. I wish I could be there with you."

Tascha's voice is soft now. Soft the way it was for so many years when Max used to have sudden, inexplicable panic attacks, soft like when things got heated with a group of customers at the outdoor supplies store and he needed to be soothed. Soft like it used to be in bed in their moments of intimacy. Soft the way it used to be when she spoke around campfires.

Max imagines her arms around him a moment, then shakes his head. "Where are you, anyway?"

"In a rented house. We tied up Doctor Tescar in the basement. It's strange how natural that felt, like I'd done it before."

"You have done it before, Tascha. We all have. I remember all of it. It's crazy."

"That would explain why it's so easy. How about you, Max? Where are you?"

"Just outside Terrytown. I've been sleeping in my van."

"Max, hold on a second, will you?"

Tascha speaks in hushed tones with someone he presumes to be Frin.

"Max? Is your van soundproof? Can we use it to store Doctor Tescar? We need to get him in the same room as the monkey. That's how we'll get some real answers."

"Tascha, you can let Doctor Tescar go. We don't need him. The monkey will release your memories if that's what you want. Just, be careful what you ask for. I'm not in a good place right now and I wish I could just forget."

"Is that what you want?"

Max hesitates. "I don't know."

"Because if we have Tescar and the monkey, we can go either way."

"I don't want any harm to come to the monkey. She's

kind. I think she may be wise, too. I mean, she's got a wise face."

"Don't get attached to a monkey, Max."

"She's really nice. I've only met her once but I already have a really good feeling about her."

Tascha snickers. It's a mean, hard snicker. Max hesitates. "Tascha, what do you intend to do?"

"Max. We do what the fuck we want. Look don't move, OK? And don't get the monkey out yet. Wait for us."

"What do you intend to do, Tascha?"

"Whatever it takes."

Tascha hangs up.

...

Max stops by the caretakers' building on his way to the monkey's enclosure. Jine is sitting, cleaning his equipment.

"Hey Jine," says Max, poking his head through the door. "Just on my way to see that river monkey again."

Jine nods. "Good for you." He stops cleaning his equipment and waits for Max to go on.

"Jine, tell me... You mentioned how people get weird in front of its cage sometimes. Has anyone ever become violent? Has anyone ever tried to attack the monkey?"

Jine's face scrunches into suspicion. "No."

"Thanks," says Max, "Anyway, bye." He backs out of the building and heads toward the monkey's enclosure.

A few minutes away from the enclosure, Warin's greeting appears in his mind.

"Hello, Max."

It should feel weird, the voice inside his head, but it feels familiar. Warin's voice is warm and indulgent.

"Hello, Warin," he mentally projects back. "I doubt I'll be able to get you out today. The caretaker Jine suspects something."

He walks around a clump of bushes and the enclosure comes into view. He waves to the monkey. Warin waves back from the mouth of the cave.

"I remember you, Warin. I remember you used to pad around the premises at the Institute. We all thought you were just a cute monkey. We thought maybe you were there as a kind of animal therapy."

Warin laughs, hops toward to the fence. "That's actually the exact reason I was there, for the calming effect of a furry animal."

They meet at the fence. Max sticks two fingers through the opening in the fence and shakes the monkey's spindly fingers.

"I told Tascha about you. Might have been a bad idea. I think she might be coming here to kidnap you. She's gone some kind of crazy."

Warin's fingers and voice tense. The tension has its own sound, a vague background whine.

"I know," says Warin. "I let her go. Released her from the spell. From your couple. I broke your couple up. I'm sorry. It was the only way of getting you to find your way back here. My intention was to let you to live out your lives as a happy couple, to stay here my myself, trapped in this enclosure. But then, something has happened and now I have to get out of here. I have to correct or prevent something. Max, I need your help. You know, of all the kids I strung together into couples, you were my favorite."

Max smiles at being the favorite. He clears his throat, struggles to repress proud tears.

"You released Tascha remotely? You've been maintaining all the couples, all this time?"

"I can see the webs, the connections, in my mental space. Whatever I've built, I can reach out and un-build."

Max looks around. "Can you reach into anyone's head?"

"No. Something was different at the institute. Doctor Tescar had you all on a combination of drugs that rendered you mentally pliable to reinforcement. It facilitated your mental rehabilitation and retraining. When these drugs were in your systems, I could see your minds glow. I could wander into them at will. I could leave doorstops. I don't know how to describe it differently. I could put placeholders that allowed me to come back later. I left those placeholders in every one of you. It's like a network. I can't speak to you until you're physically close to me, but no matter how far you are, I can see into your minds. Every one of you."

"I should explain all of this to Tascha."

"I released Tascha. Has she really gone crazy?"

"She secluded Doctor Tescar in some basement, tied him up. Pretty sure she's been torturing him. Hope I'm wrong about that."

"That does sound crazy. Max, get me out of here."

Max looks around. "I don't know how I'm going to do that. I can't just walk up to the fence with a wire cutter and let you out."

"You can if you come here after nightfall."

"That makes sense. OK then, I'll come back at nighttime. It's not like I've been sleeping, anyway. The memories make it difficult. I see faces. I remember things being crushed. Torn."

"Sorry, Max."

"Was it really necessary, though? Couldn't you just have asked me for my help?"

"You needed it, Max. Without Tascha around, you have to build yourself back up. To build yourself up you need the past. Think of it as a house."

"So Tascha isn't coming back to me."

"Who knows? I released her, I can't see her anymore. I didn't know what she'd bounce back to. You could probably predict that better than I could."

Max nods. "OK. I'll come back tonight and get you out of here."

"Thanks, Max."

Max walks back along the path. From his peripheral vision he sees Jine standing by another enclosure. Jine has been watching them the whole time. As Max heads back to the entrance, Jine catches up to him. Max turns to face him.

"You were just standing there in front of the enclosure," says Jine. "It looked like the two of you were talking."

Max shrugs. "That's stupid. I don't speak monkey. And neither do you, apparently."

He waves and leaves the zoo.

...

Max scales the zoo wall after midnight. It's a brick wall, high enough to keep out most kids, but has no barbed wire or encrusted shards of glass, in case kids try to scale it. Max relies on the strength of his fingers and toes to get up, his shoes attached together by the laces hanging around his neck. He puts his shoes back on when he gets on top of the wall. He lets himself hang off the edge, holding on to the top, sways a moment, then lets himself drop down. He falls instinctively into a crouch position, turning to survey the surroundings.

'This is ridiculous,' he thinks. 'No one is going to shoot at me.'

He smiles at the muscle memory. He stops smiling when images of actual battlefields come flooding back to him. He shakes his head violently, slaps himself a few times across the face.

'All I'm doing is breaking into a zoo. This is nothing. I wouldn't even get arrested for this. I'd just get thrown out of the zoo and someone would tell me indignantly not to come back.'

He lopes toward Warin's enclosure, stops near the surrounding bushes. It's the last spot with cover before the open space in front of the enclosure. He crouches in the bushes, patting his side bag containing the pair of mini wire cutters. They're a cheap import and the outdoor equipment seller in him disapproves of their finish, but it's all he could find in Terrytown and they only need to serve once.

He scans around the enclosure. With inexplicable certainty, he knows that Jine is somewhere close, waiting.

He mentally projects to Warin.

"I'm here, Warin. Let's get you out of here."

There's a moment of silence before Warin's reply.

"What? I'm not hungry."

"Warin! Wake up!"

"Oh! Max, it's you. I'm awake. What was I thinking, not hungry? Haha! OK then, where are you?"

"Not far from the enclosure. I need you to look for Jine. He's somewhere around here, I'm sure of it."

Another moment of silence. "You're right, Max. I can see him, sitting in the bushes, drinking from a vacuum flask. Fascinating guy, Jine."

"Where is he exactly?"

"Directly in front of the enclosure."

"I'll go around the back."

He backtracks down the path, finds an opening in the bushes that leads to a clump of trees. He slows, gingerly avoiding stepping on dead twigs and fallen branches. The ground is littered with empty beer bottles, cigarette butts, junk food wrappers and condoms. It's a favored spot for teenage wall hoppers holding late night get-togethers in the zoo.

He reaches the back of the enclosure and scales the wall of the small building. From there he walks over the roof to the edge of the enclosure's wired section. The wire is fixed to the building with long screws. The entire enclosure is wired off in an enclosing rectangular prism. He squats on the wire, feeling its slight bounce. He peers ahead of the enclosure until he spots Jine sitting in the bushes. The metallic surface of Jine's vacuum flask gleams from the light of the lamp posts spread out sporadically over the grounds.

Max pulls the mini wire cutters out from his side bag.

"Warin," he projects. "Look. Up on the roof."

"I see you."

"I'm going to cut out a hole in the wire. Can you climb to the roof to get out?"

"Of course I can. I'm a monkey." Warin sounds offended.

"OK, here goes. Once you're out, run for the wall. My van is parked close by."

Max opens the wire cutters and applies them to the wire. He strains. The metal wire compresses.

"This is going to be harder than I thought," projects Max.

"Take your time. Jine hasn't noticed anything."

Max squats down even further, gets an overhand grip on

one of the wire cutter handles. He grimaces and pushes. The wire gives and snaps suddenly, emitting a loud twang, a pure note with a springlike tremor that resonates through the air and echoes loudly off the far walls of the zoo.

In the distance, Jine jumps to his feet and sprints toward the enclosure.

"I can see you, Max!" shouts Jine. "I can see you! I'm going to lock Peaches away!"

As he runs, he rips a set of keys from his back pocket. He reaches the enclosure, unbolts the door, slips inside and slams it behind him.

"You cheated at arm wrestling!" shouts Max from the roof. "I should have won that, you fucking grip-choosing cheater!"

He opens the wire cutter with difficulty. The blades have become slightly twisted and their inner surface is already nicked from cutting the first wire.

"Fucking foreign crap!" he shouts.

"I'm not foreign!" shouts back Jine. He lunges toward Warin. Warin bolts toward the far wall and latches onto it, scrambling up quickly up to the top of it. Her hip problem seems to be forgotten in the rush of the action. Jine runs over to the wire wall and begins to scale it himself.

"Peaches!" shouts Jine. "Come down here!"

"How stupid do you think that monkey is, Jine?" Max strains and snaps another bit of wire. A loud twang bursts into the night.

Jine looks up at Max. "What are you saying, that Peaches wants to come with you?"

"No," says Max sarcastically. "Peaches loves living in a cage. You are such an idiot."

Max opens the wire cutter. There's another nick on the blades. He picks an unscathed part of the blades and applies it to a new wire.

"Incidentally," says Max, "when I said 'foreign crap', I was talking about the wire cutter, not you, Jine. I would never say that about anyone."

He strains and cuts through another part of wire. The

twang is duller this time, less sonorous, as though the wire mesh were giving up resisting.

Jine drops away from the wall. He grabs a broom from the entrance of the building, reaches up and tries to prod Max with the end. The broom strikes the bottom of Max's boot soles. Max laughs down at him gleefully.

"Who has the upper hand now, Jine? Huh?"

He cuts through another wire, which only emits a dull snap. He pulls back the section of wire to reveal a hole big enough to let the monkey through.

"Let's go!"

He runs back to the building roof, crosses over to the end, and jumps off the edge. Warin swings across to the enclosure top, avoids Jine's swinging broom and wriggles through the hole in the wire, following in Max's direction.

Jine stares dumbfounded a moment, then shouts "Fuck!" He runs back to the enclosure door, ripping out his keys. He fumbles for the right key. He shouts again, "Fuck!"

He gets the door open and runs out, circling toward the back of the enclosure. Max and Warin are nowhere to be seen.

14

"So," says Rialdy, "do you ever take your monkey out for a walk, to get some air?"

Eva laughs at the suggestion. "Gimmee is not a dog."

"Where does he poop?"

"He uses the toilet. I told you, he's a very smart monkey."

They lie in bed a moment, saying nothing for a moment. The early afternoon sun is filtering in through the bedroom window. Rialdy, closer to the window, turns to stare out of it. From his angle he can't see the forest, only the blue sky traversed by a single, stark tree branch entering the window's view from the left. It looks like a gnarled hand pointing west.

"My husband will be back this week," says Eva. "If we want to see each other, it will have to be at your hotel."

Rialdy nods. "Will you bring your monkey?"

Eva laughs again. "No! I will not bring my monkey! I'll be coming straight from work when we meet."

"This may sound like a strange request, but could I have your monkey for a few days? I've come to the realization that monkeys are perhaps my favorite animal. I'd like to adopt one for myself when I go back to Canada, but I'd like to make sure I'm up to it before I commit. I'd feel terrible if I were to get a monkey, then maybe Tace might be allergic to monkey hair and I'd have to abandon the poor thing by the side of the Trans-Canada highway. It'd be like abandoning a dog, except that I wouldn't have to contend with just those sad dog monkey eyes. The monkey would be waving sadly at me. I'd be looking at that in my rear view mirror, forcing myself to accelerate away from a living embodiment of my own insufficiency."

"Do you want to get a river monkey, like Gimmee?"

"Maybe, I don't know. Would you leave him with me for a few days?"

"You're going to keep him in your hotel room? I don't think you're allowed to do that."

Rialdy nods. He looks out the window.

"Just for today, then. Lend me your monkey for the day."

"I thought you'd be spending the day with me?"

Rialdy turns to her, embarrassed. Having just asked to keep Gimmee for the day, he can't pretend to be busy with work.

Eva stares at him a moment before letting her face break into a smile. "I'm only teasing you, Rialdy. I have things to do myself today. Of course you can take Gimmee for the day. He's very well behaved. You won't have to worry about him running off. Why don't you have some breakfast with me before you go?"

They head downstairs. Rialdy follows her on the spiraling staircase, admiring the way her hips sway as she descends the stairs, bathrobe rippling from side to side.

Gimmee hops onto the counter as Rialdy sits down at the breakfast table.

"Eva says I can take you for the day," projects Rialdy, picking up a plate, pretending to be focused on it.

"Don't frown at the plate. It looks like you've found something dirty in it and you're too polite to point it out, but at the same time you're too socially inept to hide your reaction to it."

Rialdy drops the plate down on the table and smiles at Eva, who's preparing a pancake mix. Her hands are a blur, flying over the counter top. She breaks two eggs with a single gesture and drops their contents into the large mixing bowl with a flourish. She throws the empty shells overhand into the garbage bin from a few meters' distance. They hit the inside of the bin with a hollow thud. She returns Rialdy's smile.

"So where will you go?"

"Huh?"

"You're taking Gimmee for the day. Where will you go

with him?"

"I don't know. Is there a zoo somewhere? Animals like to stare at other animals, right?"

Eva laughs. "You could take a walk by the sea. It's a little chilly at this time of year but it's a pleasant walk anyway."

"No. I hate beaches. I don't see the point of spending time on them. I much prefer a vigorous mountain hike."

He projects to Gimmee, "Quick, tell me where we're going! I'm making this up as we go along."

"So?" replies the monkey. "You can say what you want, it's not like she were coming with us to check."

"But where are we going?"

"I'm not sharing that information now."

Rialdy turns to look at the monkey. The monkey looks away, nose twitching, looking like a bored monkey, inattentive to a conversation taking place in non-monkey language.

Eva has finished making the pancake mix and leans against the counter, arms crossed, staring back and forth from Rialdy to Gimmee. She looks as though she just asked a question and is expecting an answer.

"How're those pancakes coming along?" says Rialdy, cheerfully.

Eva's face turns slightly sideways, as though Rialdy would make more sense from another angle. She looks like she's still waiting for an answer to her unasked question.

"So hungry," says Rialdy. "I can help you make those if you like."

...

They leave the house and wait at the corner for the bus, Gimmee sitting on Rialdy's shoulder.

"When does the bus come?" asks Rialdy.

"I don't know. I never get out of the house. I know nothing about buses. I'm not omniscient, you know. I can just sometimes read minds like yours."

Rialdy nods. "So where's my mother's grave? That's where we're going, right?"

"Ichava. And no, I don't know where that is, but I do

know that's where she came from originally. I got it from your mind. Interesting how you can't access those early memories but I can. There's much, much more there. Much of it is pretty cringeworthy."

"Ichava," says Rialdy out loud. "I'll have to find out where that is. I guess we'll take the bus downtown, then find a place to rent a car for the day. I hope Ichava is within driving distance."

The bus arrives. Rialdy heads to the back, to the long sideways benches he prefers.

"That's a nice ice monkey," says a teenage boy with a serious face.

"River monkey," Rialdy corrects him.

The boy shakes his head. "No, that's an ice monkey."

Rialdy shrugs. Let the teenager have his delusions.

The teenager, looking at him, bristles at the superciliousness.

"Do you know the main morphological difference between animals that evolved for warm climates and those that evolved for cold ones?" he asks, in a tone of authority.

"No."

"It has to do with the surface-to-volume ratio. Animals in warm climates tend to need to dissipate heat more, so their limbs are be long and slim, to maximize their surface in relation to their volume. Animals in cold climates will be rounder and have shorter, bulkier limbs to retain heat."

Because the teenager is speaking in Aranacian and using technical words, Rialdy has trouble following. He frowns as he listens, craning his neck forward. He gets the gist of it, looks down at Gimmee sitting in his lap, examining his limbs. The monkey really does have short limbs in comparison to other monkeys. His body is squat and, with the exception of his long tail, leans toward the roundish.

"Is he calling me fat?" asks Gimmee. "Is that little shit calling me fat?"

"Are you sure you're a river monkey?"

"Are you sure you're human? Of course I'm a river monkey. I know where I came from. All of us were river monkeys."

The teenager is getting off the bus. He stands in front of
the side exit door, holding the vertical pole and waiting for
the bus to stop. As though he just heard Gimmee and is
deliberately contradicting him, he repeats before stepping
out, exaggerating every syllable, "That is not a river
monkey. That is an ice monkey."

"Fuck off, kid," says Gimmee, "You're ugly."

Rialdy chuckles. "You know, you have a lot of personality
for an ice monkey. Not sure personality is really needed in
cold climates though."

...

They rent a small car at the first rental place they find
downtown. It's pale blue. There's a faint smell of old man's
feet inside. Gimmee wrinkles his nose when he sits down in
the passenger seat. "We'll have to keep the windows open
for a while."

Rialdy squints at the map he got with the car. "Ichava is
pretty far." He frowns. "I don't think we'll get there before
late afternoon."

He turns to Gimmee. "Thank you," he says, solemnly.
"Thank you for doing this for me."

"This isn't for free," replies Gimmee. "After this you owe
me. And I won't let you forget it."

"What will I owe you?"

"Whatever I ask. Shake on it."

"But I don't know what I'm shaking on."

"Don't worry, it'll be reasonable. Here, shake my hand."

"I don't know what I'm agreeing to, so whatever you're
making me shake on is non-binding."

He reaches over and shakes the monkey's hand.
Gimmee's fingers, surprisingly long, curl around his hand.
The arched nails, which look like brown wood, press
against the skin on the back of Rialdy's hand. For a
moment, his hand looks as though it's been caught in a
trap. He withdraws his hand, slipping it out of Gimmee's
grip. Gimmee's hand remains hovering there a moment
before he lets it drop.

"Anything I ask for," says Gimmee.

"Within reason."

"Anything."

Rialdy shrugs and starts the car. He drives to the city gate and heads onto the four-lane highway. He turns the radio on and beats his hands against the steering wheel to pop rhythms as he drives.

"This is nice," he says. "This is fun."

"You're very creative with the way you beat the rhythm. You're a good receptor. I think you could be a professional drummer."

Rialdy nods. "You really think so?"

Gimmee laughs in a squeaky, whiny and corrosive way. "No."

"You don't think anything anyway. Apparently I do all the thinking."

They reach Ichava mid-afternoon. It's a small town, dense with one- and two-story houses that mimic one another's simplistic but warm design.

"This is nice," says Rialdy. "I don't know why you'd ever want to leave this."

"Boredom," replies Gimmee. "Yearning for bigger things. Seeing how much you can get out of your talents and abilities in the greater world."

"In other words, Canada."

He drives past the town hall. "Where do we go from here?"

"Keep driving. She loved her childhood house. She had a picture of it that she often showed you. I'll know it when I see it. Unless it's been destroyed, of course."

"So, just... drive past houses then?"

"Yes."

They drive past houses.

Now and then, Gimmee points to a house and says, "It could be that one. I'm not sure though." Each time Rialdy asks him, "Do I stop?" the monkey only shrugs.

At the end of a street, the monkey states with a note of finality, "This is it. This is the house where your mother grew up."

Rialdy stops the car and stares at it. It's unfamiliar at first. He gets out of the car, walks a few steps and looks at it from another angle. He recognizes it. He can't remember which photograph exactly, but the house is familiar.

"What do I do? Just walk up to the house and knock?"

"What else are you going to do?"

He walks up to the door and knocks. After some time, he hears a child screaming. The child's screams don't appear to be happy or frightened, rather like the child is testing what volume it can hit.

A woman opens the door. She seems grateful to talk to another adult. "Hello?"

"Hello," he says in timid, tentative Aranacian. "My mother once lived in this house. At least, I believe she did. I'm not sure. Her name was Irinanka Kossume. Is this the house of the Kossume family?"

"We bought this house from the Kossume family," the woman replies. "There was no one living here when we bought it. A woman named Kossume passed away, then the house was put up for sale by the state."

"By the state," echoes Rialdy, stunned.

"There was no legal heir." The woman appears uncertain.

"I'm the legal heir," says Rialdy. "So, in principle, this house belongs to me."

The woman hesitates. "My husband will be back soon."

Rialdy looks past the woman. The child is standing there, a little boy with some dry food remains plastered across a chubby face. He looks to be about four years old. He holds his hands behind his back. One pant leg is curled up to his knee. His socks are hanging off his feet.

"Is this your son?"

"Yes."

"I can't have children."

"Oh." She nods, clears her throat. "We bought the house from the state. We have the deed to the house."

"How are things with your husband?"

"What?" The woman's eyes register alarm for the first

time, as though she's suddenly realizing she's talking to a man who isn't completely sane.

"I'd be perfectly happy to adopt your son. I could move in here. It could be our house."

Rialdy is surprised at his own words. They're just spilling out of his mouth. "I'm a good person. Do you see that monkey sitting in my car?" He turns to point to the car. "He's my monkey. I take good care of him. I take good care of everybody."

"My husband will be arriving soon."

"You said that already. The thing is, you see, this is my house. Irinanka Kossume was my mother, and it was her house. So now it's my house."

"My husband —"

"I work for a living. I have a job."

She slams the door. Rialdy walks over the lawn and peers into the living room through the large window. The woman moves to the living room window and pulls the curtains closed.

"You're acting crazy," says Gimmee. Gimmee's voice seems to be coming from right beside him. "The police are going to come. You're a foreigner. How are you going to explain this to your employer? What will you say to Tace?"

"Shut the fuck up and stay out of my head."

"At least let me out of the car. If the police come, I want to be able to move freely."

Rialdy walks back to the car and opens the door. Gimmee hops out. "You're acting crazy, Rialdy. What is this sudden need for continuity? You've never cared about it before."

"I have a house. At the very least, the Aranacian state should reimburse me for whatever it got from selling the house."

"Let's go."

"I'm not going anywhere. This is my house. This is my heritage."

Rialdy moves back to the lawn and sits down in the grass, facing the house. The child pushes through the curtains and stares at him, pudgy hands held flat against the window. He stares at Rialdy with frank curiosity. Now and then he turns back, ostensibly answering his mother calling him away from the window.

15

They reach the van and jump in through the driver-side door, slamming it shut just as Jine reaches it. Max starts the engine while Jine pummels the window with his fists.

"Keep punching that window!" shouts Max. "Like you could ever punch through it!"

He turns to Warin. His voice drops into a casual tone. "I don't expect you could strap yourself in there. Can you maybe adjust the seat belt?"

"No. It won't go tight enough. Hurry up and get going, will you? I feel terrible for Jine out there, feeling powerless."

"Well, he is powerless," replies Max. He turns to Jine and flips him off through the window. Jine momentarily stops pummeling the window, looking flustered and powerless.

"Jine is a dedicated man, and he was always kind to all the zoo animals, even the birds. I could never read into his mind, but just from observing him it's evident that he's sublimated some violent past through his devotion to caring for animals."

"It's still a zoo, though. Basically a prison for animals."

"I don't know. The animals never seemed unhappy to me."

"Can you read their minds?"

"No."

"Well then."

Max pulls away from the curb and drives a few meters, then breaks suddenly, allowing Jine to catch up. Jine runs up to the window, then slows to a walk alongside the van as Max nudges the van forward at walking speed. Jine gestures for Max to roll down the window. Max responds by gesturing his incomprehension.

"What do you want, Jine? I don't understand. Speak up!"

Jine speaks through the window. He doesn't seem menacing, rather calmly calling for Max to be reasonable. Max accelerates a moment, pulling ahead a few meters. Jine momentarily stops, expecting the van to take off for good this time.

Max stops the van and rolls down the window.

"Giving up already, Jine?" He leans his head out the window and flashes Jine a large grin.

"What are you doing, Max? Where are you going with Peaches?"

"Peaches. Ha. Her name isn't Peaches, Jine. It's Warin."

"Warin, eh?" Jine takes a few deliberate steps forward as he speaks. "Where did you get that name from? Did you make it up yourself?"

"No. Warin told me. Warin talks to me. You can't hear her, but she communicates through the mind, in some transmission medium that's unknown to science."

"Listen to yourself, Max. You're talking like a crazy person whose parents told him in early youth that he had a vibrant imagination."

Jine takes a few steps forward.

"Well, maybe I am crazy," says Max. "Who knows these things, right? But here's some advice for you, Jine: calling people crazy will get you nowhere in life. Maybe if you were a little better in interpersonal communication, you wouldn't have to earn your living as a caretaker in a zoo."

"I like my job, Max. Do you like your job? Tell me, what is your job, anyway?"

"I own an outdoor supplies shop. I have no boss. I'm at the top of my own personal social pyramid. That's how I don't have your reflex of requiring permission for things."

Jine, now only a few steps away, suddenly sprints and lunges at the van. He thrusts a hand through the open window and grasps Max's jacket, over the shoulder. His grip is solid. Max grins and accelerates the van slightly, just fast enough to prevent Jine from getting his weight behind the grip. Jine holds on, running awkwardly, alternately sideways then forward.

"Stop the van, Max! Hand Peaches back to me and we can forget all about this!"

"Jine, Jine, Jine." Max shakes his head. "You're going to fall under the wheels of the van, Jine. You're going to get your legs crushed. Do you think your employer will be grateful? I think we can both agree you've already gone beyond the call of duty for today. Just call it a failed night and go home to sleep."

Jine lets go of Max's jacket. Max stops the van.

"Where are you going, Max?"

"I don't know yet. Warin'll tell me. We're old friends, Warin and I."

Jine nods. "I'll find you, Max."

"No you won't. You won't even get time off work to look for me."

Max hits the accelerator and zooms off. He watches Jine in the rear view mirror, standing motionless, hands at his sides.

"Poor Jine," says Warin. "You really pushed his boundaries there."

"So," says Max out loud, cheerfully. "Where are we headed?"

"The island of Wizniu. There's someone there that I have to meet. An old friend."

"Sounds great. I'm up for a little vacation myself. How do we get to Wizniu?"

"I don't know, Max. All I have is the name, Wizniu."

...

They drive all night. In the early hours of the morning, Max pulls into a roadside truck stop to sleep for a few hours. Warin sleeps too, waking up frequently to gaze out the window at the surrounding landscape, at the vehicles powering forward on the highway.

When he wakes up, Max gets himself a coffee from the shop and some cake for Warin. "I don't know what you eat."

Warin takes the cake. "Mostly nuts and fruit, but this will looks good. Thank you. How long will it take us to get to

Wizniu?"

"Are we in a rush?"

"We are. I wish I could tell you we're just on the way to meet a friend to catch up and all that, but we're actually going there to prevent him from committing a very stupid act."

"Who's your friend?"

"He's a monkey, like me."

"How do you know he's about to do something stupid?"

"We're all connected."

"Like a phone network?"

"No, not like a phone network. We've existed for millions of years. The web of interconnectedness is organic, alive. You can't compare it to a phone network."

"Well, you used the word 'web', so in a sense you're comparing your interconnectedness to spider webs."

"Spider webs are just one kind of web."

"I think spider webs are the original web."

Max, satisfied with his analysis, nods. Warin looks out the window, lost in thought.

"Max. How's your head?"

"Good."

"I mean, how're you dealing with the memories?"

Max shrugs. "Not thinking about them much, to be honest. they weighed on me a few days, then they faded into the background. They didn't stay fresh. It's kind of like reheated food. It can seem fresh at first, until it cools down again, then it doesn't seem fresh at all."

Warin nods. "Then the doctor's experiment was a success. If you can go without thinking about something for long enough, it doesn't matter anymore."

"That's not how science works. It's just me. It's what you call anecdotal evidence." Max turns to the monkey. "Can you understand that? Can you reach into my brain and read my knowledge? This is so cool."

"No. Some things are too complicated for me to understand. I guess we didn't evolve like humans, with the same requirements. We didn't have to stand up straight.

Standing straight, apparently, is a requirement for thinking straight."

"Does that make you sad?"

"No."

"It would make me so sad to think there are smarter species than me in the world."

"I'm not sad."

"So, you're my oldest friend. My oldest friend that's still around, anyhow. I never realized how close our connection was back when Tascha and I were being turned into a couple, at the Institute."

"I loved all of you. I didn't understand what the doctor wanted to do with you, at first. Then, when he got you pumped up with the medication, when your brains all started to glow, I saw what needed to be done. The doctor had you in hypnosis, in reinforcement sessions, in digitally enhanced mental conditioning. None of it was effective. I saw your minds bend a little in the way he'd intended, but then they'd just bounce back. I wasn't sure at first if any of it was really good, but I saw how your minds were scarred and filled with fear and pain, and when I understood what the doctor's blueprint was, I decided I could help. I did what he hadn't managed to do, which was to tie you together, bind your minds two by two, create this huge shared space for all of you to live in. It seemed like a worthwhile experiment."

Warin remains silent a few moments. When her voice comes again, it's pained.

"At the end of the year, the experiment was going so well that the program had to be moved to a new, bigger place. It didn't occur to me that I wouldn't be brought to that new place. I'd have resisted the move, through all of you. But then, you were all gone, the institute closed down, and I was surrounded by people who couldn't hear me. And then, I was brought to the zoo."

"Well, that sucks. But, you're out of the zoo now, so."

"Yeah. It's nice. To be out here, in the car, looking out the window at landscapes floating by, always slightly different. It's nice to be heard. This car seat is comfortable. I can feel the little bumps on the road."

"Can't you talk to your friend? The one we're going to see in Wizniu?"

"No. It's a little far. In any case, he shut me out years ago."

"Some friend that is." Max reaches out and pats Warin on the shoulder. It feels strange, so he follows it up by lightly punching Warin's shoulder.

His phone rings.

"Where are you?" Tasha sounds angry.

"On the road. This is my life now. Just driving around, being free."

"Your money will run out eventually. Are you with the monkey?"

"Maybe I am. Maybe I'm not."

"That means you are, you fucking idiot. I want the monkey. I want my memories back."

"You know I love you, Tascha. You know I always will. But I don't trust you with the monkey. Tell me, what have you done with Doctor Tescar?"

"Doctor Tescar is fine!"

"Let go of the doctor. You don't need him. You don't really want him. You're just holding on to him because it feels like you're in control of your life. This is all about control. You're basically acting like a hostage-taking anorexic."

"Oh, look at you, big psychology expert since you stole a monkey from a zoo. Is she feeding all this to you?"

"No, I've been cultivating myself these past years. You just never noticed. Maybe all our years together were a waste of time."

"I want my memories back, Max. Wait for me. Meet me. Don't punish me because our union was fake."

Max echoes, "Fake?"

"You're bitter about it, obviously. You're using the monkey to punish me for waking up first."

"Why would you call our union 'fake'? It was architected.

That doesn't make it fake. Is a house a fake cave?"

Tascha sighs. "I don't think so. I don't know."

Max waits.

"You're right, Max." Tascha sounds like she's biting her tongue, struggling to sound placating. Max finds he's placated anyway. He hesitates.

"Tascha, I know you want your memories back, and I want that for you too, and I'm sure the monkey would be perfectly happy to restore them for you..." He presses the phone to his neck to mute the sound and looks to Warin for confirmation.

"Of course," replies Warin. "For now though, we have to meet my friend in Wizniu."

Max puts the receiver back to his ear. "But first I have to know that I can trust you around the monkey. I want to be sure you're not going to get violent, the way you did with Doctor Tescar."

"Doctor Tescar is fine!"

"Where is he?"

"In the trunk! He's fine!"

"You're on the road?"

"We're looking for you, Max."

"I'm not in Terrytown anymore."

"Which way did you head?"

"Let Doctor Tescar go."

"Don't be stupid. He'll go to the police."

"No, he won't. We represent the only professional success he's ever known. He turned a group of ex-child soldiers into peaceful citizens using advanced mind conditioning techniques. If he goes to the police, it'll become known that some of his ex-patients have derailed. It would strip him of his one and only accomplishment."

The ensuing silence shows Tascha is impressed with his reasoning.

He hears Tascha muttering to Frin, "He says he won't go to the police and we should just let him go." Frin mutters something back in an uncertain tone. Tascha says, "... Not getting anything out of him anyway..."

"OK," says Tascha into the phone, "We're letting him go."

"I need some kind of proof."

"Well, if I let him go, how can I prove he's leaving without following him?"

Max thinks about it a moment.

"Have him scream at the top of his lungs. I have to hear his screams fading into the distance, that's how I'll know you've let him go. Also, give him my number so he can call me when he gets back to his office."

"OK. Then you'll meet me so the monkey can restore my memories?"

"Yes. Then I'll meet you."

On the other end of the line comes the sound of doors opening and slamming shut. Footsteps on gravel. A trunk being opened. He hears Tascha's voice, "Watch his head." A thud. Tascha and Frin laughing together. Tascha explaining the situation to Doctor Tescar in a low voice, adding, "You'd better scream, and you'd better scream loud and not stop, because if you do, we'll just come pick you up again and put you back in the trunk..."

A few moments later comes the sound of Doctor Tescar screaming. It quickly fades away. Max is disappointed by how quickly it faded.

"You have a shit phone, Tascha."

"Will you meet me now?"

"Not now. There's something we need to do first."

"What?"

"We have to go somewhere. It's a few day's drive. We have something to do over there. We'll contact you when we're done."

"Are you kidding me, Max?"

"That's how it's going to be, Tascha."

"You are punishing me. You hate me, Max. You say you love me but really you just hate me."

"I don't hate you, Tascha. I love you."

"I think you hate me, too."

"No. I don't hate you. I am enjoying this, I'll admit that

much."

He hangs up. Tascha calls him right back.

"Max? Don't hang up like that. There are some things I want to say to you."

"Whatever you say, Tascha, I'll just suppose you're saying to convince me to bring the monkey to you."

"Fine. But I'll say them anyway."

Max waits.

"Something happened to me a while back. It was very sudden, Max. It happened almost overnight. One day you were there, familiar, my rock, and the next day I didn't recognize you on a deeper level. You were still familiar, but it was as though I wasn't part of that space anymore. I know this doesn't make sense ..."

"It does make sense, actually." Max looks over at Warin, who's still looking out the window.

"I thought I'd grown out of our relationship and that I was probably ready for new adventures, a new beginning in my life. But Max, I can't be whole without you. You will always be the only thing keeping me sane. I love you, Max."

"Is Frin hearing all of this?"

"Yeah. He's driving."

"Describe his facial reaction to me, would you?"

16

Rialdy and Gimmee leave the car parked in front of the Kossume house and walk to the local cemetery.

Rialdy gazes out over the length of the cemetery, at the iron grave signs floating over the green grass.

"How do we find the Kossume plot? I doubt they're organized in alphabetical order."

"That wouldn't make sense anyway," replies Gimmee. "They'd have to dig people up and move everyone down one plot every time a new body arrived."

"I was making a joke."

"I know. I'm just reading your own thoughts in response to your joke. I didn't get the joke itself. I'm a monkey. I don't know what alphabetical order means. I don't even know how to read. I recently learned how to use a toilet. I still don't like it."

Rialdy points to the cemetery welcome center. "There must be some kind of map there."

The building door is locked. Rialdy peers inside through the windows. All the lights are out.

"They're closed. We'll just have to walk by the plot one by one until we reach my mother's."

"I'll wait here," says Gimmee. "Wave when you find it."

The only way through the plots is over a dirt path. Rialdy walks slowly, taking in the rusty iron grave signs. Many signs bear quotes from the dead. It's a staple of Aranacian culture to remember the dead from their wittiest remarks. He wonders if his own wittiest remark is yet to come, if he'll get wittier as he grows older, or if he's already said it and perhaps no one remembers it.

'Maybe my wittiest remark was told to someone I don't see anymore.'

He hears Gimmee guffaw, reminding him that the monkey can hear all his thoughts.

Some of the quotes are written in a local dialect and he struggles to decipher them. They often end in a long series of exclamation points, substituting energy for wit.

He finds the Kossume plot. It holds ten markers.

'My ancestors.' Rialdy is oddly touched. The last marker is his mother's. 'Irinanka Kossume.' It bears no quote.

'That would have been my job had I been here, to recall the grave marker quote that everyone would remember her for.' He hears Gimmee grunt noncommittally.

He waves to Gimmee, who immediately takes off toward him. Gimmee doesn't follow the path. He hops wildly between the plots, sometimes bouncing right up on the iron markers and soaring on to the next one before jumping back down. Rialdy watches the monkey approach, wondering if he's purposefully acting stupidly wild in this place of devotion and contemplation.

"So, you found it," grunts Gimmee when he draws near. "How does it feel?"

Rialdy shrugs. "I don't know how to feel. Cheated, mostly. My mother's life went on here and she never invited me to visit, never bothered even to send me her address. She just packed her suitcase when I turned 18 and came over here, shutting the lid on her life in Canada. She must have felt as though her duty was done."

"You must have been quite a disappointment for that to happen," says Gimmee.

Rialdy turns to the monkey. He feels very close to kicking him.

"I'm just telling the truth as I see it," adds Gimmee, sensing his thoughts. "If both of you had shared a closer bond then she'd have stayed, obviously. I'm not saying you're a disappointment in absolute terms, only that she had expectations of you that you didn't fulfill, and probably couldn't because those expectations were never spoken aloud. So, you know, calm down."

"Disappointment," echoes Rialdy. "What does that even

mean? Invisible strings tethering you to some point that you can't even feel."

Gimmee grunts. "So are we done visiting your mother's grave? Do you have enough material toward some kind of vague future closure?"

Rialdy shrugs. "I don't know. This is just a place, a bunch of iron markers, and beneath the earth the remains of bodies of people who were once alive. Probably a lot of calcium and phosphorus left, and whatever other minerals bones are made of. Even less material for those of them who were cremated. Mostly just carbon." He trails off, looking upward and blinking rapidly, the way he did as a child when he was nervous or scared.

Gimmee grunts again. "So are we done?"

Rialdy looks at the monkey. "Yes. I guess we're done."

"Good." Gimmee turns and hops off toward the cemetery entrance. "That means we're off. This concludes half the transaction. I helped you find your mother's grave. The next half is you helping me get home to my island."

Gimmee hops brightly, bouncing off plot markers, sometimes twirling around their support poles, swinging by a hand, by a foot, by his tail. His lack of respect for the dead is now patent. They're alone in the cemetery, so Rialdy can only suppose that this indignity is committed for his sole benefit, as though through calculated transgression Gimmee were imparting some lesson about irreverence, a lesson about being free, about being able to ignore dead people and memories.

Rialdy sticks to the path, cutting no corners, respecting the narrow line of dirt that gives the dead their space.

...

They go back to the ex-Kossume house. A large man is sitting on the hood of the rented car. He has a fat face and a short beard. A vein throbs at his temple. Rialdy goes over to the driver-side door, hoping to leave without making any trouble. The man slides off the hood and steps into Rialdy's vital space as he unlocks the car door.

"Hey," says the man in Aranacian, "were you talking to

my wife earlier?"

"I was," replies Rialdy. He unlocks the door, pulls it open.

The man places a hand on the door and slams it closed. His breathing is labored, partly from being angry, partly from being fat and angry.

"My wife said you proposed to marry her. She said you were acting strangely. With my son, right there with her."

"Yes, I had a strange moment. It's strange, seeing this house."

Rialdy keeps his gaze cast downward to avoid further angering the man. The man grips Rialdy by the collar and pulls his face close to his own.

"Listen to me —"

"— Please let go of me —"

"— You're going to get out of here and never show your face here again, do you understand? You filthy piece of marsh mud."

"My mother owned this house. I'm the legal heir, I could take this house from you if I wanted to."

The man hesitates.

Rialdy adds, "Did your wife tell you that?"

The man keeps his hands on Rialdy's collar, but his grip lightens.

Rialdy pursues, "My guess is that she didn't tell you that. My guess is you didn't have to bid for the house when you bought it. There was some kind of deal. You know someone who made it possible for you. This is the first time you own a home and you're proud of it."

"Get out of here," says the man. He reaches out and pats down the front of Rialdy's shirt.

"You can keep your house," snorts Rialdy. "I'll have some coffee before I go, though. Have your wife make it while you give me a tour of the house. I just want to see it. My mother lived here."

The man hesitates, then appears to resign himself. "Come inside," he says, waving Rialdy in.

"I'll wait here," says Gimmee.

...

Rialdy cradles a large cup of coffee and follows the fat man around the house as he shows off his projects and belongings. He built all the furniture himself, and as he describes each piece to Rialdy he grows friendlier and more animated, finding in Rialdy an unexpectedly attentive and appreciative audience, as opposed to his wife. Rialdy, happy to give the man a little recognition, asks questions.

They make their way outside where foundations have been laid out next to the house.

"An extension," says the man. "To have more room. My wife and I are planning to have another child."

"Wow," says Rialdy, "you just never stop. You're a real work horse."

The man's eyes sparkle with pride. "This is where I'm laying my roots. This is where I'm making my life. I could never grow tired of building it, for me, for my family."

Rialdy sees it for the flagrant and transparent manipulation that it was, the appeal to the universal respect for the devoted family man. He sighs and hands his now-empty cup to the man. "I'm off."

"You won't make trouble?"

"No." Rialdy walks toward the blue rental car, where Gimmee sits placidly on the hood like a statue, in exactly the spot where the man was sitting when they returned from the cemetery.

"Let's go," says Rialdy, walking around the car. Gimmee follows him with eyes only, then hops off the hood.

They drive back to Wizniu, arriving shortly after dark. Neither of them said a word on the way. Gimmee breaks the silence as they draw near Eva's house.

"Your next task is to pick me up here and get me into your workplace."

"What? Why?"

Gimmee looks out the window. "Because I asked."

Rialdy rings Eva's doorbell. Eva's husband answers the door. Rialdy smiles, points to Gimmee. "I've come to return the monkey."

"You must be Rialdy. I'm Ioan, Eva's husband."

Their eyes meet. Rialdy wonders how much Ioan knows or suspects of his wife's extramarital activities.

"Come in," says Ioan, taking a step back and waving him in.

Gimmee hops inside. Rialdy follows warily.

"This is going to be fun," says Gimmee. "You're going to pretend like you don't know the house. Try to look around a lot, as if everything were new and surprising."

Eva comes to greet him in the living room. "Hello!" she says, with a little hand wave in front of her heart. "Did you enjoy having Gimmee with you?"

Rialdy clears his throat. "Yes." He looks around the living room, trying to look like he's never seen anything in it.

"It's a mentally difficult task," he projects to Gimmee. "It's like pretending you can't read."

"I really can't read," replies Gimmee. "I don't have to pretend."

Rialdy nods solemnly. "You have a really nice place here."

Eva looks embarrassed. Ioan shrugs. "It's a place to live," he says.

"Would you like to see... the kitchen?" asks Eva.

Gimmee hops onto Eva's pant leg, latching on then pulling himself up her leg, behind her arm, up onto her shoulder.

"Oh, show him the whole house!" proposes Ioan. "Are you thinking of settling down in Aranacia, Rialdy?"

"No, no... I'm just thinking of getting myself a monkey, like Gimmee here." He points to the monkey sitting on Eva's shoulder. His gesture pans over Eva, though, and he stops mid-gesture, troubled, letting his arm flop back down.

Eva points to the kitchen. "The kitchen is my favorite room in the house. It's where I spend my best moments."

"Not the bedroom?" laughs Ioan. He looks at Rialdy and laughs even harder. Rialdy smiles benignly. All three walk into the kitchen together. Eva points out the kitchen window. "I really like the view from my window. It makes me forget that I'm doing dishes."

"I have to go," says Rialdy. "I have to bring the car back before..." he looks at his watch and shrugs.

"You haven't seen upstairs," says Ioan.

"Well," says Rialdy, trying not to look at Eva, "when you've seen one bedroom, you've seen them all."

"Smooth," remarks Gimmee.

"I hope you enjoyed your day with Gimmee," says Ioan. "Now you know if you want to get one for yourself."

"Yes," says Rialdy.

"No," says Gimmee's voice.

"No?" asks Rialdy, aloud.

"Sure," says Eva.

"No," repeats Gimmee.

"What?" says Rialdy, aloud. He blinks quickly, trying to focus.

"Tell her you don't know yet if you want a monkey or not," says Gimmee.

"Actually, I don't really know," says Rialdy. "I'm not sure."

"You'll think about it, then?" suggests Eva.

"Why do you want a monkey anyway?" asks Ioan.

"Why?" echoes Rialdy.

"Yes, why do you want a monkey?"

"I don't know."

"Monkeys are fun," suggests Eva. "They can be very affectionate. And, they can be trained to use proper human toilets, so there's very little cleaning up to do."

"Tell them you're going to pick me up tomorrow," says Gimmee.

"Tomorrow?" projects Rialdy.

"They sometimes go crazy though," says Eva, "with the curtains and toilet paper. They can really trash a place if they're in one of their weird moods." She turns to kiss Gimmee, who dutifully touches his lips to hers.

"Can I pick him up tomorrow?"

"Tomorrow?" asks Eva.

"Tell her to drop me off at work," says Gimmee.

"Why do you want to come to the workplace?" projects Rialdy to Gimmee.

"Tell her."

"Just drop him off at the office when you come by," says Rialdy.

"I can't bring an animal to work," says Eva. She blushes as though there were some added explanation that she can't provide in front of her husband.

"Well, OK," says Rialdy.

"Don't take no for an answer," admonishes the monkey. His voice sounds gruff, dark, and it echoes as though from inside a cave. It's disquieting. It seems to Rialdy that the monkey could choose to reverberate even louder if he wanted to. He hasn't yet pushed the volume on his mental voice or magnified its effects. Rialdy feels a slight chill.

"I'd like you to bring him anyways, if it could be managed."

"She won't dare say no," explains Gimmee. "Not in front of her husband. She needs for this conversation to have zero drama."

"So, tomorrow then?" asks Rialdy.

Eva nods.

"You can go now," says Gimmee.

"It was nice meeting you," says Rialdy, shaking Ioan's hand. He turns to Eva and shakes her hand, too. "Thank you for lending me your monkey. It takes me some time to make up my mind. I'm a very cautious person."

Eva's hand is limp. She shakes his hand mechanically and without warmth. Rialdy nods to both of them, then leaves the house.

He hasn't reached the car before Eva's text appears on his phone. "What do you want with my monkey?"

He replies, "Just want to be sure that owning a monkey is what I want."

Eva texts, "You're a strange man. I'm starting to wonder if I was right to trust you."

...

He drives back to the city center. He decides to keep the

car, stopping by the car rental agency to prolong the contract. He drives around the island, radio blaring, not wanting to go back to the hotel. He should call Tace, but he doesn't want to hear her voice, doesn't know what to say to her.

He parks near the beach and walks along the boardwalk, hands in his pockets, listening to the sound of waves beating against the sand. A single group of words rolls around in his head, 'no past no future no past no future.'

On the drive back he accelerates sharply, flooring the accelerator, making the engine roar and the wheels screech. Just once.

17

Jine asks for a few days off work to look for the monkey. Dina, his boss and the zoo director, smiles at his reason for wanting time off.

"You're going to look for Peaches? That's how you're planning on spending your time off?"

"You think it's ridiculous," says Jine.

"I don't," assures Dina, waving the notion away. When she first took on the job, she thought Jine ridiculous, pathetic. But she no longer does. When she watches him from her office making his rounds, when she sees the care he brings to each animal, the way he talks to every single one of them, even the birds, she's moved. Only through the proxy of Jine's care has she been able to feel any affection for the animals. She still sees them as manageable assets, but she allows that perhaps Jine is also right, in this devotion which takes hold of him so strongly that now, with an animal lost through no fault of his own, he nevertheless wants to take time off work to find it.

She hasn't mentioned it to Jine, but she's already looking for a new monkey to replace Peaches.

"How are you going to look?" she asks. "Where will you start?"

"I've searched for the van. I managed to get the first three numbers off the plate as it was speeding off, which was enough to trace it back to Ishak prefecture. The guy, Max, said he owned an outdoor shop, so I've collected the phone numbers of all the outdoor shops in the region. I've been calling them up. I ask for Max each time."

Dina nods. "Any luck?"

"I have ten numbers left to call. I'm confident."

"What makes you sure he wasn't just making it up, about

working at an outdoor shop?"

"He was trying to impart some lesson about being self-employed to me. He wouldn't make it up in that kind of circumstance. He was bragging."

"People lie when they brag. Bragging is a form of lying."

"If he was lying, he'd have told me he owned a chain of outdoor shops. He wanted to beat me with the strictest truth, to win honorably."

"Well, Jine, let me tell you, in your job here you accomplish much more than that guy ever will in his. If he has to be self-aggrandizing, it's because he doesn't feel good about it."

"You probably don't believe what you're saying, but thank you for saying it anyway."

Dina arches her eyebrows in surprise. She knows Jine isn't stupid, but she can't help but continually fall back on to her bosom-held idea that anyone who isn't acting as pure homo economicus, in a professional setting, is delusional and open to be exploited.

"Take an extra day," she says. "On the house."

"Thank you, Dina."

"And, bring Peaches back for us," she adds.

"I just hope Peaches is still alive." Jine shakes his head. "Did you know there are places in the world where they eat monkeys alive? It's a weird ritual that has to do with bonding with whatever creature you're eating, and monkeys being so close to humans, it's the closest it can be to a bidirectional exchange without resorting to cannibalism."

"That's disturbing," says Dina, her mouth stretched at the edges as though she feels bad about inventing the ritual herself. Jine's fear for Peaches is palpable.

"I'm going to make a few more phones calls. When I saw I had only ten numbers left I stopped because I knew that once I get to the end of the list, I'm out of leads. But then I could simply visit Ishak prefecture, check out all the outdoors shops."

"What other motive would there be for kidnapping a monkey? Besides eating it alive?"

"I don't know. People go crazy around Peaches. She has a weird effect on people. I've seen people start crying all of a sudden while standing in front of her enclosure. I ask them about it and they say, 'I just remembered something, that's all.' It can't be coincidence though, there has to be something else. It was even more intense with Max. I saw him fall onto his back and clutch his head like he'd just had the biggest headache ever. He was just like the others who had sudden moments of revelation in front of the monkey enclosure, but he was different, too. He was the only one I've seen who seemed to recognize that Peaches had done something to him, that he was under some kind of influence. He didn't seem afraid or angry about it, either. He'd just undergone some powerful, unpleasant emotion, triggered by Peaches, yet he didn't seem to blame her for it."

"Huh," says Dina. "Almost as though he were familiar with Peaches. It's totally possible, you know. Peaches was part of the Institute for Behavioral Research next door before they closed their doors. We took her in because the head of the Institute brought her over."

...

Of the ten phone calls Jine has left, he reaches Tascha on the seventh. The outdoors shop is registered to her mobile phone number.

"Yeah," answers Tascha.

"Hello? Is Max working today?"

"What's this about?"

"I need to contact Max. There is a Max working for your shop, right?"

"Could you tell me what this is about?"

"I work for a zoo, in Terrytown, and —"

"We're not a zoo, we sell outdoor equipment."

"I know, it's about a monkey, Peaches, that disappeared from the zoo a few days ago."

"I don't even know where Terrytown is."

"Well, if I could talk to Max."

"I don't know any Max."

"You said though —"

"I asked you what it was about. Are you at all interested in outdoor equipment?"

"No. I just need to speak to Max."

"Well, good luck to you. I don't know anyone named Max."

Jine waits. Tascha waits. They're both silent for a long moment. Jine supposes that, if she weren't lying, she'd be either filling the silence with words or cutting the conversation short. It's suspicious that she's doing neither.

He waits some more. Tascha still says nothing. Every drawn-out moment of the silence becomes added confirmation that Tascha does know a Max.

On a whim, Jine adds, "Did Max come from the Institute for Behavioral Research?"

"Why would he do that?" asks Tascha.

"Do... What? He did come from the Institute then?"

"I said I didn't know anyone named Max."

"I can tell you know who and what I'm talking about. If I were to contact the Ishak business directory and find out who owns your outdoor shop, would one of the owners be named Max?"

"Did you say Max?" says Tascha in a dead tone. "I do know a guy named Max. I said I didn't, though, because Max owes some people money and he's afraid someone's going to beat him up."

Jine sighs. "May I please speak to Max?"

"Of course," says Tascha. "I'll put him on."

There's a long pause. Jine hears a series of unintelligible mumbling voices. Then a man's voice says, "Yes? This is Maxorian speaking. How can I help you?"

"Max?" says Jine.

"I prefer 'Maxorian'. 'Max' is so common."

On the other end of the line, Frin holds his chin up to pretend to be someone else. Tascha is gesticulating wildly at him, criticizing his performance harshly but wordlessly. Frin turns his back to her, still holding his chin high.

Something in the voice is off.

"Bullshit," says Jine. "You're not Max."

"Maxorian, please."

"This is bullshit. Put the woman back on. Tascha."

Tascha comes back on, audibly flustered. "This is getting tedious," she says. "You don't seem to be at all interested in outdoor equipment. So, you understand, I don't really have any interest, from a business standpoint, in maintaining this conversation. I've been polite up to now, but you're keeping me from getting actual work done —"

"Max is in some real trouble, you know. He took a monkey from Terrytown zoo."

There's a pause on the other end. "What do you know about the monkey?"

"A lot. I'm the monkey's caretaker."

"Maybe I do know the Max you're looking for," admits Tascha. "Maybe. Tell me more about the monkey."

"Well," says Jine. He pauses. "It's kind of hard to explain." He adds, "...as you may know."

"I do know," says Tascha.

"How much do you know?"

"Enough. Enough to know that the monkey can help with... what Max has."

"That you have too," says Jine. "Otherwise you wouldn't be asking me about the monkey."

"I may have it too," says Tascha. "Can it really help?"

"I've witnessed Peaches accomplish some pretty amazing things," said Jine. "But I'm afraid Max has no intention of bringing Peaches back, so you may never know."

It's a gamble, supposing that Max and Tascha aren't together on this, and further supposing that Tascha might be excluded in a way that might make her hungry and resentful.

"Max isn't like that," says Tascha. "Max is dutiful. He may not seem like it sometimes, but if there's a duty is on his list, he'll get around to it eventually."

"People change after they've experienced the Peaches' effect," says Jine. "Not always in good ways. Sometimes they completely cut off ties with their family and go into isolation."

Jine is purely inventing now, throwing together information about cults and drugs in hopes it might somehow resonate with Tascha.

"I'd like to experience what the monkey can offer," says Tascha.

"Then help me find Max. Tell me where he went with the monkey."

Tascha laughs. "Help you? You're a zoo caretaker. What the fuck do you know about finding people? Why don't you tell me what you know about the monkey and let me do the finding? Don't worry, I'll bring you back your monkey."

"I'm more than a caretaker."

"Are you." Tascha sounds like she's about to hang up.

Jine hesitates, looking straight at the wall he's facing, seeing yet not seeing the little asperities, the tiny dried drops of paint. Walls are painted without care in the zoo administration building. It's given that they have to be done over every year because they're inevitably mucked up by bringing animals. Very deliberately, he says, "Listen, what's your name again?"

"Tascha."

"Listen Tascha, whatever you're hoping to get from the monkey, you won't get if I'm not there. I make the monkey's power happen."

"Oh yeah? Wow."

"Let's just say that the monkey's power requires a certain amount of facilitation."

"And what kind of facilitation is that, you bullshit caretaker?"

"I'll keep that information to myself right now. I need you to help get me to Max and the monkey."

"I don't think I need you, to be honest."

"If I'm not there, you'll find Peaches is really just like any other monkey. Cute, furry, interesting to look at, and appears to have very human reactions at times, especially the facial reactions. But nonetheless a monkey."

"How about I give it a try without you, and bring Peaches

back to you if it doesn't work?"

"What if I told you that could backfire?"

"Backfire how? Is the monkey going to shit all over me? I'm a big girl, I can deal with things. Idiot zoo worker."

"My name is Jine. You can call me Jine."

"Oh, thank you. I was just thinking how impersonal our conversation was, and how much easier it would be to relate to you and collaborate if you'd only tell me your name."

"I just prefer that you call me by my name. That's the way I was raised, to call people by their names and not just say hurtful things for no reason."

"I hear you, Idiot zoo guy. So tell me, how does it backfire?"

"It just does, Tascha. I don't understand it any more than you do. Like you said, I'm just a caretaker in a zoo. But you see, I'm an observant one, and I've noticed what works and what doesn't work."

"You're boring me, Jine."

"Listen, Tascha. before I worked at the zoo, I worked next door, at the Institute for Behavioral Research. Peaches was my responsibility."

"Again, bullshit."

"It's not bullshit."

"I was there, Jine. Max was there. You weren't."

"It was a big place. My job was to be invisible."

"You still sound like you're full of shit, Jine, but I'm going to pick you up in Terrytown. You'll ride in the backseat at first. If you don't behave you'll ride in the trunk. How does that sound?"

"I... OK."

"Believe me, Jine, you'll want to behave. There's blood in the trunk. It's not mine and it's not Frin's. It's from someone who's not in the trunk anymore. Do you want to know where this guy is, the guy whose blood is in the trunk?"

"I don't think it matters, at this point."

"Don't get smart, Jine. Don't start to think you have any talents beyond being a caretaker for zoo animals. If you start to think you have unrealized potential, you'll take risks that you don't want to take, and you'll get hurt. You'll get broken, and beat up, and some things we'll break in you will never work again properly the way they used to. The instant you get into my vehicle, you cease to be in control of your life. I'm be in control of your life, and getting safely back home depends on you doing what I say, answering my questions truthfully, and basically being a good boy. Can you be a good boy, Jine?"

"I can be a good boy. I just want to get Peaches back. That's it."

"I'm glad to hear that. You've made me a happy woman today, Jine. So, this is how it's going to work. We're going to drive by the Terrytown exit, and you're going to be waiting there, by the trees near the exit sign. You'll be wearing only a tshirt and your underwear. That's how we'll know you're not armed. We'll stop the car, and you'll come forward and turn around twice, with your arms out, to show us you're not hiding anything. If anything seems wrong, we'll drive away and you'll have taken off your pants for nothing. Otherwise, you can get in."

"I can't just wait under an exit sign in my underwear! It's cold out."

"Well, tough. Once you're in the car, you can wear some of Frin's clothes, but not before."

"How do you know this guy Frin and I are the same size? His clothes might not even fit me."

"They probably won't, and also I don't care. We'll be by the exit in an hour. Be there, in your underwear. See you later, Jine."

18

They reach the bridge to Wizniu in late afternoon.

"There it is," says Max. "We're here." He parks the van by the side of the road, a few hundred meters away from the bridge.

Warin wakes up, her eyes fluttering open. She appears lost a moment, then she focuses on the bridge.

The structure is huge, hulking, massive, but also elegant in its own way. An array of cables hook up at regular intervals on both sides of it, each tethered to one of five pillars that shoot upwards, so high that their tips appear to sharpen into distant points. The network of cables creates an optical illusion of a warped outline of three-dimensional space.

"Now that is one impressive bridge," says Max. "And all of it built to provide access to one stupid, little, insignificant island. You'd think they had so much money to waste, back when they built it."

"They must have had good reason," offers Warin. "Maybe it was a strategic post during the war." She yawns, her jaws gaping wide, showing white teeth with prominent canines. "Let's go over."

"Where is your friend?"

"Somewhere on the island."

"So, we're looking for a monkey. On an island. Can't be too difficult."

"We're not looking for a monkey. We'd never find him. What we're looking for is a place where a catastrophe is possible. Some man-made building with important concentrations of explosives or toxic chemicals."

Max nods. "So that's what you meant when you said your friend was about to do something stupid. He's going to blow something up and get a ton of people killed."

"What you have to understand, Max, is that on a whole, as a species, we're not very rational. We have logical biases that we never escape from. Humans have them too, but at least you can train yourself to recognize them. We need outside intervention, from the more level-headed members of our own kind."

Max grows pensive. "If we can't stop your friend, we could very well all die here, am I right in supposing this?"

"Yes," admits Warin. "You know, you don't have to come. You can go back if you want."

"That's not why I said it. I was just pointing out that your friend is preparing to go extreme."

"You can see why, as a species, we never took over the planet."

"I believe you. Well, let's cross that bridge. I think our starting point should be the tourist office."

...

The tourist office is near the beach. Before they've even crossed the threshold of the door, a young girl calls out to them loudly "Hello!" Then, "Ohhhhhhhhhh, what an adorable monkey, what's his or her name?"

"Thank you," says Max. "This is Warin. She likes to be scratched behind the ears." He picks Warin up and places her on the counter. The girl scratches Warin behind the ear.

"I'm actually enjoying this," says Warin, closing her eyes. "But, why did you tell her that, Max?"

Max projects, "To make us seem adorable and not have her suspect anything after I ask the next question."

He turns to the girl. "Is this island safe? Is there any danger of any particular building blowing up? Or spreading around toxic fumes?"

The girl remains focused on Warin, who dutifully keeps her eyes closed and moves her head around to accompany the girl's scratching motion, looking as though she'd purr if she was a cat.

"Well, there's always the mine," suggests the girl, "but I don't know if it's even used as a mine anymore."

"Can we visit it?" asks Max.

"No, it's not open for visits."

"So, probably still used as a mine."

"Are you vacationing here on Wizniu?"

"Yes and no," says Max. "I'm building an eco-vacation tour platform around Aranacia and looking into eco-friendly places to put on the tour. That's why I have to ask about such things."

The girl goes around the counter, over to a shelf packed with different brochures. In a practiced gesture, she collects one of each into a neat pile.

"There's never been any ecological situation in Wizniu," she says reassuringly. "You could definitely put Wizniu on your list of places to visit for eco-friendly fun." As a joke, she hands the pile of brochures to Warin. Warin takes it from her and hands it to Max. The girl laughs in surprise. "What a charming monkey!"

"Thanks. Where's the mine?"

"I'll show you." She walks out of the tourist office, holding the door open with one foot as she leans out, cups a hand to her forehead to blot out the sunlight and squints into the distance. Max and Warin walk outside. The girl points to a tall, rust-colored building at the far end of the beach. The beach slopes downward toward its base. The building looks like it's sinking into the water.

"That can't be a mine. Is that a mine?"

"The mine is actually below sea level. The building houses all of the mining-related operations. It's been there for a very long time. It's considered part of the island's heritage."

"That's it," projects Warin's. "That's where he is, or at least that's where he intends to go. I'm sure of it."

"How would a monkey blow up a place like that?" projects Max.

"With a human accomplice, how else? Just before I was shut out of his mind, I could feel the other presence."

Max turns to the girl. "Thank you." She looks from Max to Warin, appears poised to say something, then shakes her head and goes back inside.

Max and Warin walk along the beach front toward the towering, hulking mine plant. It looms higher and more monstrous as they approach.

"A human accomplice," muses Max. "A miner then, someone who can get inside easily?"

"Not a miner," said Warin. "Only Aranacian-born workers could get clearance to work in a mine." She laughs. "I don't know how I know that, but I do."

"So the accomplice isn't from Aranacia."

"He's not. He's a visitor to the island. But not a tourist. That's all I can see."

"Huh. So he's not an Institute product, then."

They stop, standing at the outskirts of the mining plant's parking lot.

"How do we get inside?" asks Max.

"I don't know," says Warin. She looks around the parking lot, at the street, at the sea behind the plant. "Maybe we don't. Maybe we wait here for my friend to appear."

"What if your friend is already inside?"

"That's a definite possibility." Warin seems to hesitate.

"Let's go in," says Max. He steps into the parking lot.

"Wait," says Warin.

Max turns to face Warin, one foot in the parking lot. "We're here, Warin. What are we waiting for?"

Warin looks out toward the sea. The sea breeze ruffles her fur, making small ripples. She squints slightly against the wind. Other than that, she's sitting still as a statue, on the low brick wall that delimits the mining plant's parking lot, like a symbolic place guardian. Max waits in silence, leaning forward, mouth hanging open. Eventually, he shuts his mouth and stands up straight. A long moment passes. Warin seems to have forgotten him, forgotten where she is, forgotten why she's come all this way. Max sits down on the brick wall beside her.

"Maybe he shut me out for other reasons," ventures Warin. "Maybe I'm wrong to imagine that he was acting from the state in which he was before he shut me out.

Maybe he was freeing himself of me and moving on."

"Um..." Max mentally clears his throat.

"Maybe I've come here for selfish reasons. Maybe I'm just afraid of being alone."

"Warin, these feelings you're having... They sound like self-esteem issues."

"Is that what they are?"

"Sounds that way to me. You want to save the world, but you're afraid of rejection, which leads you to paralysis."

"There are only two of us left," says Warin. "We're the last two. If I let him go, he might come back. If I invade his space now though... Well. He might not."

Max takes a deep breath and scratches the back of his head. "Listen, um.. Take your time."

"You go in, Max. I'll wait here."

"Alright. I'm looking for a monkey, right? That's it? Do I need to try to kidnap the monkey if I run into him?"

"No, do nothing like that. Just... Find out about him."

Max stands up and crosses the parking lot. Warin watches him as he disappears into the building with a long, confident stride.

...

Max walks up to the reception desk. "Hey," he says to the woman behind the counter. "I'm going to meet someone I know in here. I'll be right out."

The woman shakes her head. "You have to tell me what this is about, you can't just go in."

"I'll be right out, no worries." He makes a few steps toward the elevator.

"If you don't come back here I'll call security. This is a federal site requiring security clearance. If you enter the premises without clearance, you are liable for prosecution." The woman stands, her phone in one hand at head level and the other hand hovering over the dial. A name tag on her chest reads, 'Eva'.

Max walks back to the reception desk.

He clears his throat. "What do you know about a monkey left free on the premises?"

Eva blanches. Her eyes go momentarily wide before she manages to control her reaction. "Why..." she stammers, "Why are you asking about a monkey? Is there some problem?"

Her eyes are scanning him all over now, searching for some kind of official identification. Max follows her gaze down to his clothes, uncomprehending. Sensing her discomfort, his expression turns smug.

"Why don't you tell me about the monkey?" he asks.

"Who are you?"

"My name is Max, and I'm here about the monkey. You may not realize it, but that monkey constitutes a serious danger to the personnel of this plant as well as the outside population."

"How do you know about the monkey?"

"How," he echoes.

"What kind of monkey are you referring to?"

Max notes that she's put down the phone and appears to be speaking from a place of personal rather than professional concern.

"'How' doesn't matter. Are you prepared to help me or not?"

"What kind of monkey are you talking about?"

Max considers, twisting his mouth contemplatively. "He's about this high," he says, holding an open hand at knee level. He looks down at the space he's just delimited from his hand to the floor as though the monkey were visible there. "He has a smooth, orange-tinted face and a prominent snout, with strong canine teeth. His eyes are beady and deep-set. He walks with a hop, swishing a long tail."

"What do you want with this monkey?"

"Are you prepared to help me or not?"

"First give me the information about the presence of this monkey in the plant. Who are you, anyway? You have a strange accent. Are you Aranacian?"

Max considers again. "You know what? Never mind. But know this," he says, holding up a threatening, professorial finger. Eva stares at the upheld finger with a frightened expression.

"If you let this monkey onto the premises," pursues Max, "there will be terrible consequences. Do you understand?"

"A cute monkey!" protests Eva. "An adorable monkey! What kind of consequences could there be?"

"You have no idea. This monkey has misrepresented himself from the start. He may appear innocuous, but monkeys seldom are. They hide a calculating intelligence, barely restraining overpowering urges. When we say that they're the closest cousins to man, we're not joking, and we don't mean cousins from the nice side of the family. Monkeys are capable of some pretty cold shit."

"Who are you?" asks Eva in exasperated alarm.

Max nods at her, winks, points a finger at her. "I'll be back. Get security to find this monkey, wherever he may be hiding in the plant, and be sure to put out a general warning, so anyone in the plant who spots him can immediately alert security. Move fast. There isn't much time."

"Who do you work for?"

Max winks at her again and walks backward toward the door. He senses it behind him when he's just a meter away, reaches back and pushes it open, still facing Eva. He exits.

Eva stands transfixed, until he's gone. She picks up the phone and dials Rialdy's office.

"Rialdy! What's going on? What is it with the monkey?"

"I just want to be really sure, before I commit —"

"Stop with the lying shit to me! You know something about Gimmee. You brought him to the plant for a reason!"

"Um, no. He's just a monkey, Eva."

"You're lying to me!"

A pause. "Tell me Eva, where did you get this monkey from anyway?"

"He was given to me by... someone like you. Someone who was just passing through, someone I became close to. He was leaving the country, he told me the monkey couldn't survive outside of Aranacia. I thought it strangely meaningful that you should bond with the monkey. Now I'm thinking that maybe it's more meaningful than I suspected. Where is Gimmee? I want to get him out of the building."

"I don't know where he is. He went for a walk."

"You left the monkey alone in the building? Wandering in the corridors, to do what he wants?"

"Relax, Eva."

"What if someone finds him, Rialdy? What then? They'll kill him!"

"Eva, relax."

"Fuck you, Rialdy, don't tell me to relax! I'm coming down!"

She bangs down the receiver. Rialdy turns to Gimmee, sitting on the corner of his desk.

"She's coming downstairs," he says. "She'll be here soon, so if you don't want her to find you, you should probably hide in the cabinet."

"Good idea," says Gimmee. He hops off the desk and pries open the large drawer on the cabinet. He climbs inside, exclaiming, "You have so many chips in here! Why didn't you mention it?"

"If you open those chips, Eva'll hear you. There is no way for either man or monkey to eat chips noiselessly out of a crinkly aluminum bag."

"We'll eat them later. Continue to scan the code of the software."

Rialdy scans through the code, line by line. He has never felt so alert reading code before. Every line sears into his consciousness, bringing immediate comprehension, informing him about the complex mining operations taking place far below, showing how the equipment works, the mining extraction process. It's all there. He can feel Gimmee pulling the information from his brain as he scans the code. He senses that, on some level, the monkey is both boosting his brain function and using it as an external information processing unit. He doesn't resist. He doesn't know if it's even possible for him to resist. His passivity

reminds him of the way he knows, when he goes out for
drinks, that at some point before reaching the bar he will
stop to buy cigarettes, the decision being taken as surely
and naturally as if it were an integral, planned part of the
evening.

19

Max comes back to sit beside Warin on the low parking lot wall. "He's in there. The receptionist didn't say so in so many words, but I could tell from her demeanor. He's in there and she knows about it. You should have seen her face when I mentioned the monkey."

"Can we get inside? I have to get close to him."

"No, security is tight. It's one of those national protected sites, because of the mining. I tried to warn the receptionist that there's an impending catastrophe in the works, but I doubt she acted on my advice."

Max pauses. "Maybe we should just sound the alarm."

"No," replies Warin firmly. "I don't want anything to happen to him. I have to get to him before anyone else does."

"Do you think he's going to go through with it today?"

"I hope not. It can't be a simple matter, so it probably requires a lot of preparation."

"You don't seem sure."

"I'm just a monkey, Max. I don't know how these things work. I haven't lived the way you've lived, interacting with people in an organization, conducting transactions with machines. You have a huge body of knowledge that I can only guess at by sifting through your mind. It's fascinating, but it's only alive in your mind. I can't pull it into my mind. My mind wasn't made to store information the way yours was."

"I only ask because if it's going to happen today, if that building over there is going to blow up, we're going to die."

"We should get inside."

"We can't."

"I don't know what to do, Max." Warin throws up her

hands helplessly.

Max stands up and wipes the back of his pants. "We'll wait in the parking lot and observe the comings and goings. Eventually we'll figure out some way to get in."

They go back to the van. Max stops off at the café, purchasing a large coffee and an assortment of food in anticipation of the long wait ahead in the van.

He drives the van placidly into the mining plant parking lot. "I'm going to park as near as possible to the water, just in case we notice some mind-bogglingly easy way of slipping inside the plant from there." He parks the van, puts a foot up on the seat, rests his back against the door and sips his coffee, observing the plant.

"We may be here for a while," he says. "The trick is to fight boredom. We have coffee, we have munchies, we have the radio. We don't want to take our eyes off the building in case your friend comes out, but we can't focus solely on it either.

"I don't have a problem fighting boredom," replies Warin. "I lived in a zoo for fifteen years. Every day was the same or very nearly so. There was nothing to do but gape back at the zoo visitors gaping at me. Jine was nice. He talked to me. But, he also talked to the birds."

Max turns on the radio. "Everything's better with music."

"At the zoo they played the same sequence of songs every day. It came out of speakers hidden in foliage on the zoo grounds. Every day the same songs, for months on end. I suppose it was chosen to prevent people with a seasonal pass from coming every day to the zoo and taking the place of per-day paying customers, because if they came every day they had to listen to all the same songs, in exactly the same sequence."

"I wouldn't have a problem with that, if they were songs I liked."

"Well, after a while, you wouldn't like them anymore."

"Did you like them?"

"I don't appreciate music the way you appreciate music, Max. I can't hear a song and enjoy it the way you do, because it was recorded by humans for humans and it uses rhythms attuned to the human body and heart rate, and the music itself is made to resonate with the human psyche. But, if there were people around, even people whose minds I couldn't read, I could still pick up on songs' vibe through them. It didn't matter if they even liked the song or not, I'd receive some distillate of the music through their minds, and I could sometimes enjoy that."

Max nods. "Do you dance?"

Warin blushes. Max would be incapable of explaining how he knows that Warin is blushing, but even with their imageless mental connection, he can feel her blush.

"I don't think I've ever danced," admits Warin.

"It's really simple. I'll demonstrate."

Max pushes up the volume on the radio, then begins to follow the beat of the song by bobbing his head forward. He pops his shoulders out left and right while tapping on the steering wheel.

"Can you feel that?" he says. "That's the feeling of reaching out with your whole body into humanity's common emotions."

Warin bobs her head forward a few times. "This is silly. I know there's only you and me in the van, but I feel silly."

...

A few hours pass by. Now and then, Max bursts out "There must be a way in there!" or some variant. Warin stares placidly out the window. When she blinks, her long eyelashes descend slowly, then gracefully back up again.

"Those ore boats that dock on the building, from the sea," suggests Max. "Maybe there's a way in from one of those."

"The docks behind the plant are shut off by iron bars," points out Warin.

"You could get through, though."

"Once I'm through, how would I get into the main building? I need you for that."

Max scratches his chin thoughtfully. "We can't just sit here waiting. Can't you just enter discreetly, you know, creep along the walls and swing along the ceiling or something?"

"No." Warin looks out the window and doesn't appear willing to provide an explanation. It occurs to Max that Warin might be older than he assumed.

"How old are you, Warin?"

"I'm not sure, exactly. I've seen many generations of people, if that helps."

Max whistles. After a moment he asks, "I'm wondering something, Warin. I don't know how long you've lived, but you've been holed up in a cage for a decade and a half."

"It was OK."

"You were living in a cage, Warin. Yet here you are, wanting to save the humans that locked you away, that forgot about you."

"Not everyone forgot about me. You didn't forget about me, Max. I mean, you did, because you were conditioned to, but then you remembered. I'm not here out of love for humans. I'm here to prevent Gimmee from killing. It's different. If he does this, there's no going back. There's no peace left for him if he does this."

"Well, I won't pretend to understand."

"But you do understand, Max. It'd be the same for you. You did some terrible things as a child soldier."

Max nods. "The worst was piloting the cruiser ships, the utter, wanton destruction as they descended on the Canadian wilderness. I held the controls in my hand and the voice of my captain came over my earphones, screaming at me to shoot. Below I could see children running, some of them my age..."

Warin turns to him. "What?"

"There was another boy in the barracks, probably the same age as me. He and I had an intense rivalry. We often fought, actual fistfights that ended with scuffed knuckles and bleeding noses. He won all the fights at first, but as I grew as a soldier and a pilot, I began to gain the upper hand, eventually earning his grudging respect."

"Max —"

"It all seemed so normal to me, at the time, what I was doing…"

"Max!"

Max turns to Warin. The monkey is staring at him fixedly, her face a furry mask of alarm.

"What?"

"Those aren't your memories, Max."

"Yes they are."

"Tell me about your parents."

"My father was a humble fruit salesman. He got up every day at three o'clock in the morning to tend to his fruit stand by the side of the highway. He was a very honest man and he never sold bad or spoiled fruit to any customer. He often had a few words of wisdom for people if he sensed inner turmoil in them, he'd tell them things to appease their troubled mind …"

"That's not your father. That's a story from a comic book. Can you not see the difference, Max? I can see your real memories, they're right there for you to reach down and pick out."

Max pursues in a voice of quiet despair. "My mother was a high-powered executive in an electronics firm. She piloted a project for a new generation of hybrid man-electronics soldiers…"

"That's a comic book, Max. It's not you. This is not your story. High-powered executives do not raise children with fruit salesmen in real life, the cultural divide is too large. Your real story is underneath that memory."

"I'm pretty sure this is my story. Canadians are reputedly good at bridging cultural divides."

"It's a made-up story. I don't understand. I opened the doors inside your mind. You should have all your memories back. I should have checked. This is disturbing."

Max grips the steering wheel of the van, hard enough to whiten his fingers. His breathing grows hard and angry. "What…" he starts. "What…" He shakes his head, shakes the steering wheel. He strikes it with an open palm, sounding the van's horn. He swings the van door open, slips off the seat to the ground and walks around the van. Kicks a back tire, making a whining sound in his throat. "What can I do, Warin? What can I do to get back a sense of myself?"

"I'm so sorry, Max. I opened the doors in your mind, so you should have the memories. I can see them there. They're there for the taking. There are no barriers. I don't understand why you can't access them."

"Obviously, you're not a doctor. You're just a monkey with some kind of mental power." He kicks the wheel again. "You're an amusing pet. But you can't help me. Maybe no one can."

"Max, I'm so sorry. I'm so sorry."

Max walks around to the passenger side and peers inside at Warin. Her eyes are sunken, contrite. She places a hand against the window glass. Her spindly fingers rest lightly against it, the fur pressing against the glass, showing neat flow patterns.

Max laughs. "So what! So fuck it! Maybe life is just what I make of it today, right now. Maybe this sense of myself is just a luxury that I think I need but that I don't really need at all."

"I don't know, Max. I know I need a sense of time's passage to function."

"Well, Warin, at least I remember you. Come on, let's get into the plant and find your friend." He opens the door of the van and waits for Warin to get down.

"How are we going to get inside?" asks Warin.

"We're going to take a walk around the back. You're going to go through the bars and observe the back entrance closely. There must be some button you can press to open the gate for me. Then we'll just walk inside and pretend we have business there."

"Will that work?"

"We can try it. That's all we can do. Come on."

"I don't think it's a good idea. Someone will probably question us about what we're doing there and we won't be able to answer properly."

"We can't just wait here doing nothing, Warin! That building is going to blow up and everything around it too! Come on, let's move!"

Though the van door is open, Warin looks out the front window. She seems to be observing the ocean.

"It won't happen today, I don't think," she says. "Let's just wait for Gimmee to come out and then we can reason with him."

"You are so fucking useless! You are such a fucking useless monkey! Do you know that? Are you aware of that?"

"I'm sorry, Max. You know, the comic book you're basing your life story on does come from your childhood, so you do have some of your past left, though it's not really your past, more like a common generational memory. I could describe the memories I see within you though, if that's what you want. Maybe then you could grasp them."

"Why are we here, Warin? What are you doing just fucking sitting here?"

"Gimmee will come out. Then I can reason with him."

"You useless fucking monkey! You pathetic excuse for a.... whatever the fuck you are!"

Max turns and walks briskly toward the edge of the parking lot.

"Where are you going, Max?" says Warin.

"Can't you tell? Can't you read my mind?"

"You're angry, I can see many images flowing around and into each other, but I can't see the root of your decision. Ah, now I do. You're going back to the café. That's a wise decision. Just sit down, get yourself a beverage and calmly..."

"Get the fuck out of my head!" Max projects violently. Warin's voice silences immediately, as though a switch has been thrown. Max strides off, not looking back, leaving Warin to try to shut the heavy van door herself.

He reaches the end of the parking lot and jumps over the delimiting low brick wall. Maintaining his forward momentum, he runs toward the café nestled between the parking lot and the tourist office.

"Fucking monkey," he spits out as he reaches the café entrance. He has one hand on the door when he hears someone call to him, "Max."

He turns. A van, of the exact make and color as the one he rented, sits parked in front of the café. Frin grins at him from the passenger window. Beside him, leaning forward from the driver's side, one hand still on the steering wheel, grins Tascha.

"How...?" says Max. The answer hits him before Tascha even says it.

"Online banking statements. We tracked you to this island, effortlessly. This is the last place you came to, just a few hours ago. How's the coffee here?"

Max considers, then shouts, "The coffee fucking sucks!" He lets go of the door handle, spins on his heel and starts to sprint toward the parking lot. Behind him he hears the van engine roar alive, the tires screeching as Tascha pulls away from the curb, then brakes, pulling into reverse to turn the van around.

He hops over the parking lot wall. His foot catches on the top of it. 'How,' he thinks as he falls, hitting the parking lot asphalt with his forehead, hard. Tascha's van pulls alongside the parking lot, moving quickly ahead of him. The van's side door is open. Max looks up to see Jine, kneeling on one knee, holding it open.

"Jine?" Max gasps, perplexed. He scrambles to his feet and resumes running toward the parked van, whose passenger door is still open. "Warin!" he screams. "Warin!"

20

Eva bursts into the office. "Where is he?"

"I told you," replies Rialdy. "He went off for a walk."

"Where? Where did he go? You have to help me find him. There was a man at the front desk asking a lot of questions about him."

Gimmee stirs. "What's this?"

"Asking questions about Gimmee?" echoes Rialdy. "Why?"

"Ask who it was," snaps Gimmee.

"I don't know why he would ask about Gimmee," says Eva. "Rialdy. I don't want to lose my job."

"Was it a security guy? Did he spot Gimmee on a security camera?"

"No! It was just a strange man who walked into the lobby. He didn't introduce himself, he wouldn't tell me who he was or who he worked for. I can't lose my job, Rialdy, do you understand this?"

"Well, you know, you're overqualified for reception work. Why did you give up your scientific career in the first place?"

"Because I hate science! Show me which way Gimmee went."

"Just, you know, down the corridor."

"Ask about the man!" thunders Gimmee. "Who is he!" The voice is loud enough to blare inside Rialdy's mind, reverberating, jolting. He is assailed by a wave of dizziness. He is suddenly aware the power that the monkey holds, a capacity to hurt him if he wants to. For the first time since meeting Gimmee, he fears the monkey's power.

"Who was the man who asked about Gimmee?" asks Rialdy.

"I told you!" says Eva, "I don't know!" She hurries out of the office, looks left then right in the corridor, chooses left and walks away. The sound of her heels clatters down the corridor.

From the cabinet comes the unmistakable crinkling noise of a bag of chips opening, followed by chips crunching. Fast crunches indicating small, nervous bites. It would be cute if the monkey hadn't just jolted Rialdy's mind. He reaches down and pulls the cabinet door open. From the top tray, Gimmee stares up at him, munching.

"You know what?" says the monkey. "We have all we need here, let's head down to the mine."

"What are we going to do in the mine?" asks Rialdy. "How is this related to getting you home to your island?"

"This is something I need to take care of first, before I go away forever.

"What, though? What is it that you need to do?"

The monkey deliberately tears apart the bag of chips. The chips rain down onto the cabinet drawer and around it, crumbs spraying the carpet.

"That is what I need to do." says Gimmee, "Only, imagine that instead of the bag of chips, it's the mining plant. We're going to blow this whole place up."

"Why? Why would we do something like that?" Rialdy projects it in a tone of dismay, but he's feeling something else too, a certain glee at the prospect of the building exploding, toxic chemicals blowing over the island, affecting masses of unsuspecting people.

"I'm doing this for a man I once knew, who was my friend before Eva took me in. That's something you should know about us ice monkeys, we don't have many friends, but the friends we have we care for deeply. So this man, my friend, a guy by the name of Alman, came to work in this very plant. He was working downstairs in the mining facilities. He was caught in the same trap you are, exposed to the toxic chemicals. It did more to him than render him sterile, though. It made him sick. Some kind of disease that developed from deep within his body. I don't know anything about medicine, but I could tell that he wasn't going to heal from this disease. He left me with Eva. He used to fuck her too. He was a good man, Rialdy. Like you. You're a good man. Too good to think of doing what needs to be done, which is to turn this plant into dust."

"I don't want that."

"Yeah, you do."

"No —"

"I'm not making these emotions up, Rialdy. I got them from Alman, and I'm getting them from you, and it's enough to do something about it. It really works out well too, because Alman knew which machine does what downstairs in the mine, and you know how they work inside, and the alerts were all there in the code, kindly showing us which buttons to press to induce overheating in the plant."

Gimmee picks up a few chip crumbs from the base of the cabinet drawer tray and chucks them pensively into his mouth. "Ready when you are."

"We can't do this."

"We can't not do it, either. This plant is just going to go on sterilizing people with genetic potential and making others sick. It's the rational thing to do, just accept that a few people need to get hurt now to save many more down the road. It's an ethical dilemma that is solved in your mind, Rialdy. The greater utilitarian good. I'm getting this from your mind, not mine, and I can see that you agree with it. So let's stop wasting time and just go."

Gimmee clambers out of the drawer and hops toward the door. Rialdy glances down at the carpet, at the scattered chips.

Rialdy doesn't see how he could argue with information culled from his own mind. It'd be tantamount to arguing with himself. He also can't deny his glee at the prospect of blowing everything up. He follows Gimmee out the door, down the corridor toward the staircase leading to the mine.

Eva is nowhere to be seen in the corridor. Gimmee sits in front of the staircase door, waiting for Rialdy to push it open. He reaches it and hesitates a moment with his hand on the door. "Push it open," prods Gimmee. Rialdy pushes it open.

They descend the staircase down to the mine. The orange soot caking the walls is now hauntingly familiar. Rialdy doesn't avoid it this time. He doesn't hug the middle of the staircase or try to avoid touching the wall. He hops down the stairs with one hand dragging over the dirty wall, welcoming the toxicity, feeling tough. Gimmee hops down the stairs in front of him, a blur on each staircase, then suddenly motionless when he reaches a landing and waits for Rialdy to catch up.

He doesn't know how it is they're going through with it. He suspects that, given time enough to think about it, he'd simply turn and head back to his desk. He follows the monkey now, drawn to the creature's power, his disregard for rules, his freedom, his willfulness. They hop down the stairs, the monkey flitting down swiftly and easily, Rialdy with his long, careless strides, delighting that his feet always land on a step and not the edge of a step. He feels rather than sees the steps as his feet meet them. He could go down these stairs with his eyes closed if he wanted to.

They reach the bottom landing and stand in front of the door leading into the main chamber. "That sign warns of toxic environment," Rialdy points out, jerking his chin toward the sign above the door. "But to the outside world and the media, the mine denies there's any link to worker sterility. You have to wonder if they didn't put this up here as a point of pride. As in, 'we care more about belonging to this place than to our descent.'"

"Exactly," agrees Gimmee. "For sure."

Rialdy pushes open the door to the main chamber. At the base of the metallic stairs, the same controller he met last time is standing there, in his protective hard cap and mining overalls, monitoring numbers on screens. He doesn't turn as Rialdy descends the stairs.

"This isn't where we'll be intervening," warns Gimmee, "but if that guy sees us go inside the mine he'll sound an alarm."

Rialdy nears the bottom landing. Hearing the rush of footsteps behind him, the controller turns around, too late. Rialdy leaps the last set of stairs and kicks him in the chest. The controller slumps down, winded. Rialdy kicks him in the face again and again, until the man stops moving. He stares at the controller's prostrate form. Horrified.

"What the fuck are we doing here?" he asks. He's not sure that he's asking Gimmee.

"Do you want to trash this plant or not?" replies the monkey. "This is life. You're either making victims or becoming one yourself."

Rialdy remembers the kind, sympathetic way the controller had spoken to him when Rialdy had shown he wasn't aware of the plant's toxicity. He hadn't gone out of his way, but there'd been kindness there, spontaneous and freely offered. That same man now lies unconscious at his feet.

"I don't know about this," says Rialdy.

"We're not going back now," replies Gimmee. "The only way out is forward."

Rialdy looks back at the staircase leading up to the exit door.

"There's no way back!" thunders Gimmee's voice. The voice reverberates painfully inside Rialdy's mind. Even after it's passed, he can't hear his own thoughts for a few moments. His gaze blurs. In the aftershock of the monkey's voice, he's overcome with dizziness. His gaze comes back into focus once more, on the dirty, massive, scraped metallic exit door.

He feels a sudden enveloping apathy. The staircase seems impossibly steep, heading impossibly high up. The thought of going back, of entering the stairwell and having to climb ten, twenty, thirty floors up... It's exhausting. He suspects that this is Gimmee's doing, that the monkey is somehow subtly affecting his judgment, changing the numbers on his internal gauges just enough to alter his worldview, controlling him through positive and negative reinforcement. He doesn't formulate the thought in words: Gimmee would perceive those. He's aware that if he's to break away from the monkey's grip, he has to do so without divulging his plan, without formulating it in words.

The monkey sits hunched over, waiting.

"OK," says Rialdy. "Let's go." He kneels beside the man he just kicked into unconsciousness. The controller is coming to now, shifting his position. Groaning.

"We don't have much time," says Gimmee. "Unless you feel like finishing the job here, we have to move. This guy is going to wake up and sound the alarm. Look at him, dutiful older worker. The old ones have real dedication. It goes beyond seeking professional advancement. They have real loyalty to the company. It's a second family for them. Are you going to hover above him like that? Maybe you want to take his pulse? Offer him a hot beverage?"

Reluctantly, Rialdy steps away from the controller and moves toward Gimmee. His right foot is numb from kicking the man's hard head. He kicked him artlessly, connecting with his toes. His body is trembling, adrenaline coursing through his veins. As he reaches Gimmee the urge arises, unbidden, to kick the monkey in much the same way. It'd feel more natural somehow, to kick an animal rather than a human. Because it's Gimmee, it would feel good.

The monkey senses the thought. "We can settle accounts later. But of course, you owe me for this. I'm doing this for you too, you know."

"You don't really intend to go back to Indonesia, do you?"

"Indonesia? Oh, hehe, no. I'm not from Indonesia. I couldn't even find Indonesia on a map. I can't even read a map. I can't do anything, really. I'm useless in nature because I never lived in it. I depend on humans like you to be susceptible to my voice and charm."

They reach the end of the chamber and the series of tunnel openings. Gimmee chooses the far right tunnel, without hesitation, as though he knows the mine well. They enter the tunnel just as a group of miners are coming out.

The men are wearing blue overalls and hard caps, same as the controller in the main chamber. Their faces and hands are caked in brown-orange soot. They stop walking when they see Rialdy and the monkey coming toward them. One of the men appears poised to challenge Rialdy on his presence in the mine.

"Nod to them and keep walking," says Gimmee. "Don't slow down."

Rialdy nods to them. One of the men moves to bar his path. Gimmee hops past them.

"What are you doing here without protective gear?" asks the miner.

"Software verification."

"You're exposing yourself to toxic chemicals."

"I've been working in this building for months. What's the difference?" He grimaces toward the other men, calling for their complicity in mocking the leader. One of them snickers.

The man is undeterred. "Where's your identification? Where's your pass?"

"Look," says Rialdy. "I left all that with the controller. I'm just going in for a few minutes." He turns and points to the tunnel entrance and beyond, to the main mine chamber. The man hesitates.

"I'm not going to stay here and argue with you," adds Rialdy. "I don't want to spend any more time in here than I have to."

"Why is there a monkey with you?"

"Toxin detection. Better than any electronic detector. That's how we work in Canada."

"Oh! You're Canadian! I want to go live there someday. Quit my job in the mine."

"It's a beautiful country," acquiesces Rialdy. "Anyway, see you later."

He moves on, glancing at his watch. He feels the eyes of the group on his back as he catches up to Gimmee. The corridor veers right. As he turns, he glances back. The miners have reached the main chamber and exited the tunnel.

"They're going to find him, if he hasn't already woken up," says Gimmee. "We have to run now."

They move through a series of corridors and reach an elevator. The door is caked with soot and looks like it hasn't been used in years. When they press the button, however, the doors whistle open.

"Five stops down," states Gimmee. Rialdy presses the button. The elevator lurches, creaks, then begins its descent with a sickly whine.

They emerge on a local control floor, in a large chamber with machines set against the walls.

"What is this place?" asks Rialdy.

"Testing machinery. No one uses it outside of tests, but we can connect to the real machines from here if we override the fail-safes."

"How do we do that?"

"You know the codes," says Gimmee. "They're hard-coded into the control software. Look into your memories, everything is there."

"Oh, the unit tests. I assumed those were just software tests."

"No, they connect to real machinery."

Rialdy looks around at the machine panels. Gimmee points to one. "That one," he says. "That one can open the emergency valves. Do that while overheating the pre-extraction modules and the mine will flood with enough air to ignite the local mintesium piles."

"How do we do that?"

"We know how to do that."

21

Max sprints toward the van. From the corner of his eye he can see the other van pulling ahead of him, speeding toward the parking lot entrance.

'She's going to get to Warin. She's going to hurt her to get to her memories. She's going to torture her like she tortured Doctor Tescar. She won't be satisfied with whatever she finds.'

He stumbles and runs on. "Warin!" In the distance, Warin hears. She slips out of the van's passenger door, which remained open after Max stormed off.

The monkey looks at him. Max waves both arms frantically, pointing to the approaching van. "Run, Warin! Get out of there!"

Warin bolts in direction of the water. "No!" screams Max. "Not that way!"

He watches as she runs toward the water in her awkward, lopsided gait.

'She has nowhere to go. How can she not see that?'

Tascha's van has entered the parking lot and heads straight for Warin, covering the ground between them in a few seconds.

The speeding van looks fierce, ruthless, mean. His estranged wife behind the wheel is an implacable rigid presence. If the hopping monkey were to slow down at all, she'd get run over. Max tries to remember what it was to love the woman driving the van.

'We don't love the ones who deserve it. We only love the ones who draw us into their crazy.'

He doesn't know how he knows that. Were there woman before Tascha?

He veers around a parked car, throwing himself into an

interception path. Jine drops out from the van's side door, hitting the ground running, seamless.

"Warin!" screams Max. "Not toward the sea! You have nowhere to go!"

Warin is slowing down. She hesitates before the approaching waterfront. She's reached the beach, however, and the van can't follow her any longer. It halts in the beach sand. Driver and passenger doors open. Tascha and Frin slip out, Tascha running, a few seconds behind Jine. Frin strolls around the front of the van, anticipating Max's approach, positioning himself to block him off.

As Max reaches the van, he speeds into a sprint. He takes a running leap at Frin, one foot up aiming for the head. Frin pivots on his front foot, sidestepping the blow. He puts his fists up to counter-attack, but to his surprise Max runs right past him, following in direction of Jine and Tascha.

Jine catches up to Warin and scoops her up off the ground. He folds an arm around her, pinning her arms to her body, and grips her feet together with the other hand. The sight of Warin immobilized makes Max nauseous. Behind him he can hear Frin breathing hard. He has just enough time to stop and pivot before Frin barrels into him, taking him down into the sand. His head strikes a beach rock in the exact same place he hurt it moments earlier in the parking lot. Sand presses into his face. He lifts his head, sees Tascha reach Jine. Tascha is holding a black metallic object in her hand. It takes him a moment to realize it's a gun.

Tascha points the barrel directly into Jine's face. "Thank you so much for your help, Jine. You can hand over the monkey now."

"This monkey has a name, Peaches, and she belongs in the Terrytown zoo."

"No, this is a special monkey and she doesn't belong in any zoo. Hand her over. Maybe I won't shoot you."

Jine looks around as though he suspects Tascha is talking to someone else.

Tascha steps forward. "You don't know how close you are

to being dead right now, Jine."

Jine starts, "You can't shoot —"

Tascha lowers the barrel and shoots Jine in the foot. The gunshot is largely muffled by the sea wind. A few dozen meters away, Frin and Max hardly hear it, but they recognize it for what it is when Jine topples forward.

Even as he crumples into the sand, Jine neither screams nor lets go of the monkey. Tascha lunges forward, kneeling, pressing the gun to Jine's temple. With her other hand she tugs at one of Warin's arms.

"Let go of the monkey, asshole!" Tascha presses the gun even harder into Jine's temple. "Will you just let go? Do you really want to die for your fucking zoo job?"

Jine says nothing, holds on tightly to the monkey. The bullet has punctured his right foot, leaving a hole through which oozes out blood, forming a small puddle underneath.

"Tascha," projects Warin.

"What?" says Tascha.

"Jine isn't the one talking," says Warin. "It's me, Warin."

The mention of Warin's name triggers a rush of memories within Tascha's mind. She sits back, her mouth hanging open, eyes wide and glassy. The arm holding the gun slackens, slipping off of Jine's temple. Her mouth emits formless sounds, like words from some made-up child's language. She takes a deep breath, swallows her saliva.

Jine, whose head was turned away and eyes scrunched shut expecting the bullet, now opens them, picks up his head and turns to look at Tascha. He remains staring at her a moment, trying to interpret her collapsed demeanor. Still clutching the monkey, he hoists himself to his knees, stands, sways a little, and limps off, the bleeding foot dragging in the sand as he moves.

Frin gets up off of Max's back where he was sitting and runs to Tascha he stops a few steps away from her.

"Tascha?" he calls out to her uncertainly.

Max gets up a moment later, runs, catches up to Frin, kicks him in the back. Frin groans, falling forward. Max jumps over him and goes to kneel next to Tascha, cradling her in his arms.

"You may feel like you're drowning," he croons to her, "but it goes away. Your memories might not be real, but whatever they are, they will help you."

Frin has gotten back up. He approaches. Max, cradling Tascha, throws him a menacing look. Frin stops and waits.

"Maybe," Max tells Tascha, "it's just good that we're reminded that we were alive before the Institute project, you know? That we were whole once, before we had each other. The thing is, I have to tell you now, that's all that there is. You'll get nothing more from Warin, no matter what you do."

Tascha's eyes have flickered back into focus. "I'm so sad, Max! I'm so sad!"

"I know."

"All those people!"

"Try to hold on to them. They've slipped away from me again. I don't know, maybe we're not supposed to be able to hang on to these memories. Maybe they don't fit our current brains."

He looks up at Frin. "Take care of her, Frin. I have to get the monkey back. We're here for a reason, we have to prevent a catastrophe from happening in the building over there."

"OK, that's obviously bullshit," replies Frin.

"Max stands up and goes after Jine, who first walked in the direction of the café at the end of the parking lot but then made a big circle around them. Jine is heading for the van. Max makes directly for the van, getting to it a few meters ahead of Jine.

"Let go of the monkey, Jine. She's a highly intelligent creature. She doesn't belong in any zoo."

Jine laughs, cradling Warin to his chest. His right foot is caked in wet sand. A mix of fresh and dried blood covers the top of his shoe.

"No animal belongs in a zoo, Max. It's just that the world they've known doesn't exist anymore. They need a place where they can be safe."

"That's obviously bullshit." Max walks forward. Jine transfers the monkey to his left arm and jabs with the right, standing straight, hardly winding up at all. His punch floors Max, who finds himself on his back, blinking and gazing up at the sky. He turns his head toward Jine and blinks again, twice.

"Jine, are those my clothes you're wearing?"

"These?" Jine looks down at his clothes as though seeing them for the first time. "I don't know. They were given to me by Frin."

"Why would —"

"I had to be in my underwear for them to pick me up. That was the condition."

"Well, they're mine," states Max, sitting up. "People just take things from me without asking for permission. It's really annoying."

"Why would Frin take your clothes?"

"I'm guessing he didn't have any when Tascha picked him up. Maybe that's her new thing, picking up men that don't have any clothes on and dressing them up in my clothes."

Jine moves toward the van's driver-side door. Max stands on wobbly feet.

"Jine, the monkey is sentient. I can prove it. If there's something you've only ever told War... Peaches, then I can tell you what it is."

Warin says, "That's good, Max. You're thinking straight. You're the only one here who's thinking straight."

Jine stands, his free hand on the van door, hesitating.

"What was my wife's name?"

"Warin? What was this asshole's wife's name?"

"Zue," says Warin.

"Zue," echoes Max. "Her name was Zue."

"Did she love me?"

"No."

"Did Peaches tell you that?"

"I don't need to ask Peaches, Warin, that. You're a loser, Jine. Women don't love losers."

"Fuck you, Max."

Warin says, "Tell him we can't know that, only he can."

"OK," says Max, "Warin says that only you can know if she loved you."

"Peaches will still be safer in the zoo. She's an ice monkey. Can you picture her surviving in what's left of Aranacia's North?"

"She doesn't have to be in a zoo," says Max. "She can stay with me. She needs someone she can really talk to. Don't make this about your failed relationship with your wife."

"My wife died, asshole. She didn't leave me."

"Well, maybe life didn't give her time enough to realize what a loser you are. She'd have left eventually. You know it."

"Max, you don't say things like that." Jine gazes at him fixedly, face full of hurt.

"Seriously Max, where did that come from?" asks Warin. It's the first time Warin has openly criticized him. He feels a pang of remorse.

"I'm sorry, Jine. I shouldn't have said that."

A gunshot erupts from behind them. A split second later the bullet glances off the top of the van's front hood.

"She's shooting at us!" shouts Max. "Don't shoot at us, Tascha! You'll hit the monkey! You'll hit Warin!"

Tascha advances toward them, struggling to hold the gun straight. Her feet shuffling through the beach sand, she sways from side to side as she walks. She has trouble stabilizing her arm.

"Tascha?" shouts Max. He watches as she continues to advance, acknowledges that she intends to respond with bullets and not words.

"Oh shit, shit shit shit," he says. "Jine, get in the van."

Jine stands, cradling the monkey in his arms, pensive, inscrutable.

"Jine! Protect the monkey!"

Jine snaps out of his reverie. He runs around the front of the van to get in through the passenger side. Max opens the door, slips onto the driver's seat and shuts the door just as a bullet strikes the window, shattering it. He covers his head with his hands to protect himself from glass shards. He peeks above the rim of shattered glass where the driver window was.

"What are you doing?" he shouts. "Have you completely fucking lost your mind, Tascha?"

Frin is a few steps behind Tascha.

"Frin! What are you doing? Stop her! She's going to kill someone!"

Frin shrugs and holds up his hands in a way that's simultaneously apologetic, pleading, and irritated, as though he regrets he can't help, is open to suggestions on how to help, and is resentful that it's all up to him to help.

Tascha fires off two more shots. One flies over the top of the van. Max is certain he can see the bullet flying past the windshield, though he reasons it's going by too fast to be seen. The second bullet thuds into the side of the van, puncturing the side and resonating on the metal floor vents.

Jine puts his feet up on the seat and his arms around Warin to shield her with his body. Warin discretely slips out from his right side and drops down behind the seats. It takes a moment for Jine to realize Warin is gone, then he looks around in panic. Max reaches out and tries to press Jine's head down. Jine resists.

"Put your head down!" says Max.

"Why aren't you driving off?"

Max turns to the steering wheel and sees the key is in the ignition. He starts the van and hits the accelerator. The van glides toward the water, wheels spinning in the sand. Moving in slow motion, it draws a half-circle around Tascha. Tascha calmly aims the gun at it with both hands.

"Don't shoot, Tascha," admonishes Frin, standing beside her. "You'll kill someone."

Tascha doesn't take her eyes off the van. Wheels kicking up sand, the van is moving as slowly as if it were swimming through water. Tascha's arms hold the gun, follow the van's movement, maintain the barrel trained on the van door.

"I don't want to hit Max," she admits, "but that fucking

monkey is going to get it."

"What did the monkey do?"

Tascha shoots twice before replying. Both shots find their mark, blowing out the front and back tires on the van's driver side. The van slows down even more, protruding rubber from the blown tires scooping up large amounts of sand and sending it flying backward.

"The memories, Frin, they fucking hurt." Tascha's voice ends in a sob. Her face, until now set and determined, scrunches up. Her shoulders shake. She holds out her left hand, palm open.

"Give me some more rounds, will you? I want a full cartridge's worth."

Frin produces a handful of rounds from his pocket and places them gently in Tascha's hand.

"I don't understand what you're doing, Tascha."

Tascha shrugs and sobs again. "I just want to shoot the monkey." She loads the rounds into her cartridge, one by one. "We came all this way, all this way for a jumble of memories that don't even feel like they're mine. They feel like they happened to someone else."

The van has stopped. From the driver's side, Max stares out expectantly out at Tascha.

Warin's voice comes to Tascha. "The gun will not help you, Tascha."

"Get the fuck out of my head!" screams Tascha. She pulls up the gun and fires two bullets into the side of the van.

"Stop! Stop it, Tascha!" shouts Max.

"Shut up, Max! You didn't warn me, you didn't say how it would be, like I'm being loaded with someone else's memories! What kind of husband are you?"

"I tried to get away from you, because I knew you'd go crazy and try to hurt the monkey!"

Tascha points the gun at him. "Say that again, Max. Say again that I'm crazy."

"You are! You are fucking crazy!"

"One more time? One more time, Max?" Still pointing the gun at Max, Tascha steps forward.

22

The plant-wide alarm blares and whines, the sound coming from different areas within the plant, unsynchronized, echoing.

"I must admit," says Rialdy as he types away on the dirty, dust-caked keyboard, "I'm a little shocked that I agreed to this. But you were right, Gimmee. It needs to be done. We have to reestablish some notion of order in the universe."

Gimmee fidgets. He grows still, then suddenly shifts, hopping around the room, staying put a few seconds before moving on again.

"You don't treat people like this," says Rialdy. "I was going to start a family in Canada. Canada is a good place to raise kids. In the wintertime, kids play hockey. My mother put me on skates when I was barely four years old. I have family pictures of me trying hard to stay up on the skates. My knees are buckled inward, my ankles are almost touching the ice I'm so unsure. But, you do that for a while and eventually you get the hang of it."

"Something's wrong," says Gimmee.

"This is like intentionally bad programming. Actually, it's more like writing testing code. You know all the areas where something can go wrong and you deliberately bring exactly those things about." Rialdy stops a moment, staring at the screen. "You show the program where it's straying from the truth and you force it to confront it. But then, you know it's flawed, so really you're just forcing it to confront the reality of its own flaws."

"I have to get out of here," says Gimmee. "There's something I have to do."

"Let's finish this, shall we?" replies Rialdy. "There'll be time for having fun after we're done."

"No, we have to go now."

"Well, you do what you need to do, I guess."

"Call the elevator for me, please."

Rialdy shakes his head. "No. No one is thinking of looking for us in the testing room. If I call the elevator they'll know there's someone down here."

"Call the elevator!" Gimmee's voice surges in volume, inflected with a panicked edge.

"Why?" asks Rialdy. "D'you need to pee? Just pee right here. In another few minutes it'll be the least of the plant's concerns."

"Call the elevator!" Gimmee's voice explodes through Rialdy's mind.

Rialdy stops a moment, waits for the sensation to fade, then resumes typing.

"We're going to blow the lid on the plant like a bad pressure cooker. This is my most important work. This is what I'll be remembered for. It's a pity no one will know just how good I had to be to make it happen."

"Call the elevator!" blares Gimmee's voice. "I have to get out of here! Someone I know needs me!"

Rialdy's fingers momentarily halt on the keyboard. He waits for the aftershock of Gimmee's voice to recede. He smiles. "That sounds sentimental, Gimmee. I didn't know that river or ice or whatever kind of monkey you are could be sentimental. To tell you the truth, I think you're a bit of a jerk. But, maybe I'm a bit of a jerk too. I mean, what I'm doing here requires some of that, right?"

"Someone needs me!" Gimmee takes a few running hops and springs high, landing on Rialdy's shoulder. He bites into Rialdy's neck, drawing blood. Rialdy stands straight, reaches behind his neck, grasping the monkey with both hands. He flings him effortlessly onto a testing machine along the wall. The monkey bounces off the control panel and hits the floor, swatting at the air to land on his feet before sliding to a halt.

"Calm the fuck down," says Rialdy. "Do you think you're going to fight me? You barely come up to my knees, and there's no rules, apparently. You bite me, I bite you."

Gimmee bares his teeth at him. "Forget the plant, Rialdy. Just take a little vacation somewhere in the sun. Find someone new to fuck. This need for revenge will fade."

"Oh, come on, Gimmee! Let's not fight. You're like a brother to me. Let's just get this thing done, OK? Together. Afterwards I'll take you back to Canada with me. I'll show you what real ice looks like. I'll teach you how to skate."

The elevator makes a humming sound. The numbers count down on the overhead floor indicator. Rialdy looks around the room until he spots a cluster of metal rods leaning against the wall. He runs over, grabs one and hefts it, gauging its weight.

Gimmee stands in front of the elevator, fidgeting. Rialdy moves to the side of the elevator doors, back against the wall.

The elevator doors open. Two men step out and blink at the monkey standing there. Rialdy swings the bar at the first man's head, striking him in the temple. The man goes down like a toy run out of battery power. The other man turns toward Rialdy, moving in close to take away Rialdy's ability to swing. Rialdy swings anyway. The man catches the rod with one hand and knees Rialdy in the gut. Rialdy crumples. The man falls on top of him, struggling to wrest away the rod. Rialdy feels it slipping away from his grip.

Gimmee springs on top of them, biting into the man's neck. The man screams and swats behind him blindly, rearing up, losing his grip on the rod. Rialdy shifts his hips and kicks out from under him. Scrambling to his knees, he rips the rod away. Both men stand. Rialdy swings the rod into the man's side, doubling him up. The monkey springs off the man's back. Rialdy swings again onto the man's head, watches him topple, then strikes him in the head again.

Gimmee hops into the open elevator. "Rialdy. Send me up now."

Rialdy hesitates, sighs. He reaches inside the elevator and punches the button to the top floor and steps back.

"Some friend you are," he says as the elevator doors close.

Gimmee scurries back to the main chamber. The door at the top of the stairs is open. Men in black uniforms are running through it, carrying rifles. A cluster of men hover around the injured controller, who is sitting up, holding his head painfully.

At the edge of the metal stairway, Gimmee pounces up and latches onto the support rails beneath the stairs. He swings himself up, one arm following the other seamlessly until he's hanging beneath the top of the stairs. Through the metal grid structure above his head he can see more heavy boots pounding the stairs, moving over it in a blur. He waits. When no boots have gone by for a few moments, he hoists himself up over the guardrail and plops down on the landing.

He hesitates, then runs through the doorway into the main plant stairway, moving up the stairs.

He meets another guard running down, uniformed, carrying a rifle. Gimmee stops. The man stops in front of him. He hunkers down on a knee and pats Gimmee on the head.

"What are you doing here, little friend? Are you lost?"

He pets the monkey once more before resuming his run down the stairs.

Gimmee ascends a few more floors. He hears Eva's voice calling, "Gimmee! Come here, baby!"

He accelerates up the stairs. He emits a loud, piercing shriek, mimicking panic. The panic sounds real to his own ears. He hops, feeling the blood in his ears, feeling his lungs burn. His legs fill with lactic acid, slowing him almost to a standstill. He shrieks again.

Eva runs down the stairs and picks him up, cradling him in her arms.

"My baby! I thought I'd lost you! Where were you?"

"Move it, let's get out!" he projects.

He's aware that she can't hear him. He's gotten used to conversing with Rialdy.

'I'm going to miss that idiot. I'm going to go back to being a pet with no one to talk to.'

He thinks of Warin and feels a pang of guilty panic. 'Move it!' He mentally projects again.

Eva walks up the stairs at a brisk pace. Gimmee closes his eyes, willing his heartbeat to slow down.

They reach the lowest floor with elevator access. Eva pushes through the stairwell door. They take the elevator up to the lobby.

"We have to leave the building," says Eva, in the voice she uses when she's speaking simultaneously to Gimmee and herself, as though the monkey were an extension of her. "There's some kind of an emergency. We have to get out. All of security is on alert. It doesn't look to me like an exercise. Sometimes they conduct these exercises, but you can always tell when it's the real thing and not an exercise. There's this energy in the air."

Gimmee can hear Warin, close. He can feel her strange mix of emotions, fear, anxiety, a complex mix she tries to bottle up within herself. Her restraint is familiar, it exacerbates Gimmee's flood of guilt. Guilt at shutting her out for so long while he processed the emotions left over by Alman. He hadn't expected her life might be threatened, or that she'd come looking for him.

He kicks out of Eva's arms as soon as they're outside.

"No, Gimmee!" cries out Eva.

Gimmee follows the beacon of Warin's presence, sees the van and runs toward it.

Eva runs behind him. "Gimmee, seriously! I don't have time for this! Grow up! Gimmee! Gimmee!"

...

Tascha moves in so close that Max can see down the barrel of the gun.

"Go ahead, Max, call me crazy. Call me crazy one more time!"

"Yes!" shouts Max. "You are crazy! You don't need my confirmation on that." He shuts off the van engine and stares out the windshield, sulking, one elbow resting over the gaping hole of the shot-out window.

"Max!"

"What, Tascha? What? You walk out on me, you take up with another guy, you abandon me to tend the store alone, you disappear from my life after keeping me hoping by coming with me to church, and then here you are, with all your expectations, prepared to ruin the fragile equilibrium I've found in my link to my past and my monkey companion, ruin it all because you don't fit in, because you're not included."

"Max! It feels so bad!"

"I don't care how it feels for you! I feel great. I'm calmer, I'm more grounded —"

Tascha puts the gun to the side of the van and fires two shots. From inside the van comes a piercing shriek.

Max and Tascha both freeze, their eyes meeting. They feel like children again, scared and lost.

"Peaches!" cries Jine from inside the van. "Peaches is hurt! She's hurt!"

"Now you've done it!" explodes Max. "Are you happy, Tascha? This is the kind of past we were supposed to leave behind!" He slams an open palm on the outside of the van door. Tascha jolts, takes a step back. The gun-wielding hand falls to her side.

"I'm sorry." She puts a hand over her mouth as though she just said something she'd like to take back, as though she hasn't just shot the monkey through the side of the van.

Max thrusts the van door open, narrowly missing Tascha. She takes another step back.

Frin comes to stand next to Tascha. "Give me the gun, Tascha. You don't need it right now. I'll give it back if you need it."

Frin now realizes he is an Extrapolist through and through. He hasn't been infected by any disease from Tascha's soul. He simply bound himself to her from the start of their relationship. His life is a part of hers, fulfilling his role. The role is clear to him. He opens the chamber of the gun, empties the unused rounds into his palm, puts them into his pocket and tucks the unloaded gun into his belt.

Max slides open the side door of the van. Gimmee, who found his way through an open passenger-side window, sits cradling Warin in his spindly arms. His nose twitches wildly in anger, confusion and sorrow. Warin, blood trickling from a hole in her side, lies with eyes slowly blinking. Her face shows no sign of pain recognizable as such by the humans around her.

"There's a veterinarian at the zoo..." suggest Jine, eyes wide in shock.

"The zoo is far away," cuts in Max. "Try to think outside your caretaker box."

Eva stopped running a short distance away. She approaches slowly, uncertainly.

She peeks into the van.

"Looks like you found yourself a friend," she starts. She sees the blood and her eyes go wide.

An explosion erupts from the plant, followed by two more louder explosions and the screech of gas tearing through metal. A high pitched whine emerges, grows louder even then the explosions, then narrows into a whistle. Gas plumes rise from the sides of the building. People exit in groups from the front and back of the building, running, gesticulating with flailing arms, shouting orders. A few stop a short distance from the building, others run without stopping. A few go straight to their cars in the parking lot.

Eva's gaze moves numbly from the plant to Gimmee, silently asking if this is his doing. Gimmee returns her stare, silently shrugging.

"I have to help if I can," says Eva. She turns to Max. "Can I leave my monkey with you?"

Max nods. Eva turns back to Gimmee. Silent words pass between them, something like a goodbye, a good-luck, and an acknowledgment that they didn't know each other anywhere close to how they thought they did.

Max grabs hold of the van door handle. "You're riding in the back, Jine. Try to stem the blood flow. You're a caretaker, do your job taking care." Jine glares at him and is about to say something but is cut off by the van door sliding shut.

"We're getting out of here," Max tells Tascha and Frin. "We're going to find a hospital."

"Go to a vet," suggests Frin, pointing toward the smoking plant. "The hospital is going to be full of whatever's happening here. Anyway, they won't treat a monkey in a hospital."

Max looks at Frin, sighs, opens his mouth, closes it, then arches his eyebrows. "That's a good point. OK, we have to move."

He gets behind the wheel, turns on the engine, and starts to move forward before feeling the resistance from the sand in the blown tires. He smacks himself in the forehead and steps out of the van again.

"We're going to have to switch vans. You shot out my tires, so we're taking your van."

"Actually, this is our van," says Tascha. "Your van is still in the parking lot."

Max looks curiously at the van. "Why get the same van as I did?"

"It was so if we had to ask anyone if they'd seen your van, we only had to point to this one."

"Oh." says Max. He runs toward the parking lot.

Eva heads back to the plant. The massive building looks like a wounded giant. Aranacian legends of giants fighting animal gods flit through her mind. She wonders if she hadn't seen in Gimmee some element of Aranacian mythology when she first agreed to keep him. She wonders if Rialdy is inside, and if he is, whether he's still alive.

23

The smoke plumes rising from the plant feed a growing cloud that hovers in the sky above.

In the test room, Rialdy has stopped typing. He stares at the screen with a blank expression. The extraction gasses have been released, the burners have been overheated. All that's left to do to trigger the explosion is expose the mintesium to air. But, he doesn't remember the next step.

'What a mistake, letting Gimmee go like that. He'd know how to jog my memory right now. It's nice, working in a team. I enjoy it. I should do more of it. I should learn to trust people more and work with them hand in hand.'

He pictures Gimmee's spindly, furry hand and the claws protruding from his slim fingers.

'Gimmee has cute hands. Where's he gone? We were supposed to do this together.'

He's sure the next step is locked away inside his brain and just needs him to relax to be lured out again. He closes his eyes, takes a few deep breaths and waits. Nothing comes. His mind is blank. He can't even picture the code or the code comments that describe the mechanisms he's been controlling through the testing machine. Sighing, gets up and goes over to the elevator, ignoring the sound of the guards banging on the door of the storage closet where he locked them up. He thought they'd stay out for some time, but after about a minute they were already coming to and he had to move them into the closet to prevent them obstructing.

'Where's Gimmee gotten to?'

He reaches the main chamber. No one is coming in anymore, there are only people leaving. Enough alerts have been triggered to send the plant into evacuation mode. The mining section workers are filing through the exit. Rialdy steps into line and shuffles forward with the rest of them. He wonders why they're going through the main exit and not the mine worker's entrance, then it occurs to him that the alerts have shut down the mine worker's entrance.

He heads up the main stairs along with the others. The workers are in good spirits in spite of the strident alarms and having to climb up long staircases. They joke about exercise being forced on them. One man calls dibs on the elevator. A woman calls him an idiot for wanting to wall himself up in an elevator when the electricity could be cut off at any time. Coworkers laugh. Rialdy laughs too, enjoying the camaraderie, feeling included.

They shuffle out of the main lobby. Rialdy stops by Eva's reception desk, hoping to see her, but the desk is deserted. He peers behind it. No Gimmee. He leaves the building.

Outside near the entrance, people are clustered in work groups. Rialdy moves from one group to the next, trying to prolong the feeling of inclusion, but it's fading. He gives up and walks toward the exit of the parking lot, headed for the bus stop.

"Rialdy! You're OK!"

He turns. Eva is waving to him from one of the circles of people. He waves back. Eva smiles, waves, jumps up and down.

"That's him!" shouts a man in a voice Rialdy recognizes. He turns to see the controller sitting on the ground, a doctor examining his head injuries. The controller is shrugging the doctor off and standing, pointing at Rialdy.

"That's him! That's him!"

Conversations die down. Faces turn to Rialdy.

He turns his back to them and resumes walking toward the parking lot exit.

'I won't wait for the bus. I'll keep walking and get a taxi further down.'

"Stop him!" someone shouts. The shout is echoed throughout the crowd of plant employees. Rialdy keeps his back turned to them.

'If I ignore them, they'll stop. They realize eventually how ridiculous they sound, saying the same thing over and over.'

The voices only get louder though, more pressing. He feels rather than hears that some of them are now following him.

With the sea so close, Rialdy imagines the crowd as a tidal wave rolling toward him. He shifts into a run. He's close to panic.

'If I can just make it to the parking lot exit, I'll be OK. They won't follow me into the street. They'll give up.'

The imaginary tidal wave looms larger in his mind as he nears the exit. The voices now seem to be coming from multiple angry directions. Some of them are charged with authority.

He hears the gunshot, feels a sharp pain in his upper back, goes down.

'This is so unfair. I did them a favor by exposing the toxic gasses to the surrounding town. Now they'll have to do something about it. They should thank me. This would never happen in Canada. They wouldn't shoot someone in the back in Canada unless they were absolutely sure he posed a threat to the population.'

He's not absolutely sure about that last part.

He wonders where Gimmee is.

'Gimmee and I developed a real bond in that rented car. It's a special bond that develops between people who travel together. That's what companionship is, people relying on one another as they move through space and time. People moving in the same direction.'

...

Eva stares dumbstruck as Rialdy gets shot trying to run away. A hush descends on the crowd. All eyes follow the guards converging on Rialdy's prone figure.

Azgeviu and Teoko look from Rialdy to the smoking plant.

"We're going to have to warn the government about this," says Teoko. "I don't see how we can keep the plant open now. We're going to have to find new jobs." He shakes his head, staring at Rialdy's prostrate form, surrounded by the guards who stand over him like hunters after a kill.

"We really fucked up bringing that loser into the plant. What were we thinking?"

"We weren't thinking," replies Azgeviu. "We wanted a trip to Canada. It was fun too, but what a price we now pay. We might lose more than our jobs. There'll be an investigation. They'll bring up the plant toxicity. Look at that fucking cloud hovering over the plant, nagging us. We might go to prison for putting the general population at risk."

He tuts, raises his voice to address the medical staff surrounding the injured controller.

"Hey, shit-for-brains! What are you doing? That guy is fine! You should be tending to the guy who got shot."

"He sabotaged the plant!" calls back one of the medical staff.

"So what?" shouts Azgeviu. "That's a matter for the police. What do you think will happen if we let him bleed to death? Get your overeducated asses over there and see to him!"

Grudgingly, the four medical staff members shut their supply boxes and head toward Rialdy.

Azgeviu stares at the plant. "Anyone who bought a house in Wizniu will be losing money. Property values are going to plummet."

The gaseous cloud billows above the plant, still swelling from plumes rising out of windows.

"That cloud is going to head inland as soon as the wind changes," says Azgeviu. "There's no containing it now, it's out of the bottle."

The wind is already blowing it inland. The cloud shifts and swirls, dissipates at the edges, thins as it travels.

"They'll have to evacuate Wizniu," remarks Teoko. "Relocate everyone."

Rialdy, his face pressed into the ground, watches from one eye as the medical staff approach. The controller, sitting with bandaged head, is giving him a dirty stare.

'That guy must be so pissed. I beat him up, and now the medical staff are leaving him to tend to me. That's ironic. Is it ironic, though? I can never remember what irony is. This seems like irony. I hope they can save me. I don't want to die here. I don't deserve to die. I did a good job encrypting software, then I did the whole island a favor by calling attention to the plant's toxicity. International agencies will come to measuring toxicity levels. They'll shut down the plant. There won't be any more workers losing their ability to have children. In the long run, everyone's a winner. They don't seem to realize that, that in the long run I helped everyone. I didn't kill anybody. They shot me. This is so unfair. This would never have happened in Canada. I'd be a hero in Canada.'

The self-pity is comforting. Everything he did he thought he was doing for the monkey, but he now realizes that's not the case. It was Gimmee amplifying his own wishes, forcing him to act according to his own deep convictions. All of it was about belonging. Belonging to Canada, belonging to Aranacia. His visit here, the house that could have been his but wasn't, the children he was planning to have but wouldn't, all that belonging stripped away from him.

'I belong now, though. I'm a contributing member of the human tribe. No one will forget me now.'

The medical staff surround him. Hands push up his shirt and touch his back. It stings. He can't tell if they're handling him roughly or if it just feels that way because he's injured. He decides he doesn't care. He just wants them to save him so that he can go on. He's proud of himself, proud of what he accomplished.

'How many people would do it? How many people would have the balls to even try?'

The cloud swells and breathes. The plant workers look up at it powerlessly. They wait for the order to be given to go in and shut off the extraction pipes.

Eva approaches the logistics director, who's coordinating the employee roll call. He's holding a folder with employee lists that he hands out to team leads.

"Can I help?" asks Eva. "I know most of the faces, I can check to see who's outside."

The logistics director glances briefly at her. "We don't need your help, Eva."

His tone gives her pause.

"I know the faces," she repeats.

"Why don't you go check on your little friend over there?" The logistics director jerks his chin toward Rialdy.

"He's not my friend. It's complicated."

"That's all I need to know, for now." His tone is dismissive.

Eva waits, shifting her weight from one foot to another. Her scalp burns. Her face is flushed. She can feel the weight of the attention from the team leads who stand around waiting for lists and instructions.

"I can help," insists Eva.

"Get lost, Eva."

The logistics director makes eye contact with someone behind her. She turns to see the head of security standing a few meters away. She walks up to him.

"Do you want to talk to me?"

"We will be talking. Soon."

"I don't know anything about what happened here today."

"The man was seen with a monkey, Eva. Was this your monkey?"

"Yes. He borrowed my monkey. He told me he wanted to see how it was in case he wanted to get a monkey of his own when he went back to Canada."

"What I'm hearing is that you let a man get close enough to you that he was in a position to be sharing the companionship of your monkey. I find it doubtful that that kind of proximity could exist between you without you being aware of what he was planning to do here."

"Look, my life is complicated. I value openness. I don't hide from opportunities. I pursue enigmas."

"You have no business working here, Eva. You're a

source of risk, pure and simple. You should never have been working here in the first place. I've looked at your employee profile. You were too qualified to be working the reception desk. That should have been a warning bell. We'll get to the bottom of your involvement here. In any case, you can be sure you won't be working here anymore."

Eva steps away.

"Eva!" The head of security calls out. "Where is your monkey now?"

"Safe."

Eva keeps walking. She makes her way to the edge of the parking lot and sits down on the surrounding low brick wall. Some distance off lies Rialdy, tended by the medical staff. From where she's sitting, she can't see any blood.

Rialdy seemed like such a sweet, helpless boy when he first walked up to her reception desk, asking how to get back to his hotel. Just like Alman, years ago. His manner was so polite, so eager to avoid offense. She wouldn't have picked him to do something like this. But then, that lost look in his eye, the silent, aimless way about him. Maybe something stepped in and answered it, pointing him in the wrong direction. Here he is now, with a bullet in his back and no way of getting back home.

She remembers the first evening in his hotel room, the tranquil way he had sat, an invitation to being invited. She'd felt sure she could take him into her life the same way she had with Alman. She can't decide if Rialdy reminds her more of Alman or Gimmee.

'My monkeys. All my monkeys.'

She looks from Rialdy to the plant. She imagines what it'll be like to be spending time at home looking for a new job, answering her husband's questions about her plans, seeing the incomprehension in his eyes about her choice to forgo the obvious direction of going back to a scientific career.

On Wednesday evenings she'll go to bring-your-own-culture night and wait for her turn to sing. She'll listen to the other performances, get a glimpse into other people's lives, look for herself in those glimpses. She'll have too much to drink, get home and get into bed next to a husband who looks at her like she's the ghost of some past life that failed to dissipate.

She rubs her hands against the rough texture of the brick wall. She feels it chafe her skin. She'd like to peel all her skin away.

24

"We'll find a veterinarian in Iznik," says Max.

"We need to find a hospital too," replies Jine from the back seat. "I need to have someone look at my foot."

"That is much lower on our set of priorities. You can probably just disinfect it, bandage it up and be good to go."

"I think the bullet is still inside."

"Maybe the veterinarian can look at your foot after he's seen Warin."

Jine doesn't reply. He stares at the monkeys cuddled at his feet.

"They speak through their minds?" he asks.

"Yeah."

"What are they saying now?"

"I don't know. They're talking to each other. They're on some kind of private channel."

Gimmee caresses Warin's fur in soothing, regular strokes. The gesture looks touchingly human to Jine.

The van coasts along the sea line. The road rises and falls, undulating over the relief of the Aranacian coast. The sun sets over the top of the west mountain chain. As the light fades, Max worries they won't find any open animal hospital, especially not in a place as small as Iznik.

"Hang in there, Warin. We'll find someone to fix you up."

He expects Warin's voice to sound wan, hurt, or shaken. Instead, it's blurred, as though losing focus.

"I haven't introduced you to Gimmee. Gimmee is my oldest friend."

Max looks up at them in the rearview mirror. "Are you two related?"

"All ice monkeys are related," replies Warin. "We don't cluster according to common mothers though, so the concept is..." she trails off.

"Hey, anthropologist guy," projects Gimmee, "how about focusing on the road and going a little faster?"

'Well,' thinks Max. 'Bit of a jerk.'

"We can both hear you," says Gimmee.

"Fair enough," says Max. "I just thought, having only known Warin, that all ice monkeys must be wise and benevolent like her. Having met you, I'm thinking, 'maybe not.'"

"Are you guys talking?" asks Jine. "It looks to me like you're all talking."

Max peers at him in the rearview mirror.

"I have the benevolent role," explains Warin. "Gimmee is a receptor. He may appear jaded, or cynical, but he's just reflecting the signals he's been exposed to. The receptors act, the feelers, like me are a step away from action. We're disengaged. It's a role. Obviously, it comes with a burden. I couldn't willfully step in to restrain Gimmee. I couldn't take the risk of creating a conflict."

Gimmee caresses Warin's head, contrite.

"I had to stop you, Gimmee." Her voice is projecting to both Max and Gimmee. "I knew you might hate me for it, but what you were going to do... It would have harmed us, negated us."

"It really looks to me like all of you are having a conversation," says Jine.

"You can't hear us at all?" asks Max. "That's so sad. It's like you have a sensory organ you can't use. Actually, that's exactly what it is."

"I can't hear them," says Jine in a quiet voice. He pauses. "My foot is starting to hurt. It didn't before, but it's starting to hurt now."

"I'm sorry Tascha shot you," says Max. "Nevertheless, you shouldn't leave this experience thinking that's how she is. She's not like that. She's always been a capable, energetic woman. She only changed recently because Warin released her from the memory wipe. It's like cutting a steel string that has been pulled tense between two points. The sudden tension release made her lash out in different directions. But that's Frin's problem now, not mine."

"I was married, once," says Jine. "We weren't good together every day, and she was a woman who hadn't become everything she thought she'd become, and some days I think she held me responsible for that. She died very suddenly, and all those things that she had thought she'd become —"

"Could we not speak of death or dying right now?" interjects Max. "Warin's injury is pretty serious. Have a bit of sensitivity."

Jine stops talking.

They reach Iznik an hour later. Jine and the monkeys wait in the van while Max goes into a restaurant and asks around until he gets the addresses of both the local animal hospital and the clinic.

"I'll take Warin to the animal hospital," he says, climbing back into the van. "I'll drop you off at the clinic on the way, Jine."

"That's probably best. I'll meet up with you later."

"Or not. Warin's not going back to the zoo, whatever the outcome. Do you realize that putting an animal into a zoo cage is just like locking someone up in prison? These are intelligent creatures, you can't just sequester them. They need their freedom."

Jine nods. "I know."

"You have to be very careful about what you tell the people at the clinic, about how you got that bullet in your foot. You can't mention me, or Tascha, or the monkeys. If they ask how you got injured, you have to say you shot yourself in the foot, to get out of work. You're a caretaker in a zoo, they'll believe that."

The hospital is off the side of Iznik's main street. Max drives up to the emergency room entrance. He and Jine step out of the van.

"Remember, no mention of the monkeys."

"I won't. Good luck. I'll come visit when Peaches has healed up."

Max nods. He stares at his feet, shaking his head.

"Max?" says Jine, placing a hand on Max's shoulder. "Don't worry. As a caretaker, I can always tell when an animal's life is in danger. I know Warin will be fine."

"Yeah? You think so?"

"Max, I know it. Look at me."

Max looks at him.

"I know it, Max. I'm sure."

"OK, well…" Max seems anxious to end the conversation and doesn't seem to know how to.

Jine steps forward, limping on his injured foot. He hugs Max.

Max leans into the hug, then reaches out and hugs him back.

"You're a good guy, Jine," he says. Max bursts into tears. "I could have been nicer to you." He pulls away, wipes his eyes.

"I'm going to head into the emergency room," replies Jine, embarrassed.

Max nods.

"I have to get my foot seen to. Max? I have to go now, Max. I'll come visit you. Good luck to you."

Even with Warin injured in the back of the van, Max waits for Jine to hobble through the emergency room doors before he climbs back into the van.

"OK," he says, "let's find the animal hospital."

It sits at the top of a hill on the town outskirts. Max carries Warin in. Gimmee follows. As Max runs, Warin bounces up and down in his arms in spite of his effort to run gracefully.

The receptionist is pouring herself a cup of tea, standing near the lobby window away from her desk.

"Please help me," says Max. "My monkey's been shot."

"Oh, the poor thing!" says the receptionist. She immediately goes to sit at her desk. "Why would anyone do that? Shoot a poor monkey?"

"She's lost a lot of blood. Please help her. She's all I have."

The receptionist looks at Gimmee. Max follows her gaze.

"Oh, him," says Max. "He's a bit of an asshole."

"Looks like someone shot the wrong monkey," sympathizes the receptionist. "What kind of monkey is it?"

"An ice monkey."

"An ice monkey?" The receptionist frowns. "What's that, exactly?"

"Does it matter? Please let us see the veterinarian."

"I'll call Messynda in. She's at home but she'll come in. I just need to know what kind of monkey it is to inform her. If she has to operate, she has to know exactly what kind of animal she's operating on, you understand."

Max looks desperate.

"You know what?" says the receptionist. "I'll call Messynda and get her on her way. We can fill in the information once that's in motion."

She makes the phone call. After hanging up, she hands Max a book of animal classification. "Take a look at this. Find your monkey in there."

Max takes the book from her, still cradling Warin in his arms. He goes to sit in the waiting room. Gimmee hops onto the seat next to him.

"What are you?" asks Max, flipping to the book's primate section. "The veterinarian needs to know. Maybe your internal organs aren't in the same places as other monkeys. If we can't tell her precisely, it might not go well."

Warin, eyes closed, doesn't respond. Max turns to Gimmee. "What are you? Where did you come from?"

"I don't know. Warin doesn't know either. We weren't always around humans, but our mental capacities started to develop once we were exposed to them. It wasn't a good thing in all respects. We didn't know loneliness until we were able to conceptualize it." He pauses. "We came from somewhere cold. There weren't many like us. We had once been numerous, then we no longer were. We were collected by humans and brought here."

Max sees a picture in the book resembling Warin and Gimmee. He points to it. "You must be one of these.

Inranacius Timorous. It says here you're extinct. That sucks for you. You're probably the last of your line. There'll be no ice monkeys after you're gone."

"Well, that's life," says Gimmee. "It's true for everyone, in a sense."

Gimmee scrunches his eyes closed. His voice comes to Max in staggered waves. Max realizes that the monkey is sobbing.

"So much wasted time," says Gimmee. "So much wasted time focusing on vengeful sentiments. Alman's, Rialdy's. Others. I should have not cared about what those people felt, but I couldn't shut it off. So much wasted time. Time I could have been spending with my only friend."

His voice grows even more staggered before trailing off. Gimmee hangs his head. As athletic as he is, he now looks frail.

"Hey. There'll be no more wasted time, OK?" says Max. "After Warin gets healed up, you'll both come to live with me in the mountains."

The veterinarian comes in. She places a comforting hand on Max's shoulder.

"Hello. My name is Messynda, I'll be taking care of your monkey. Did you find out what kind of monkey she is?"

"Her name is Warin," replies Max. "I'd say she's an Inranacius Timorous. Look for yourself." He holds up the classification book, his finger on the picture.

Messynda takes the book from him, frowning. "Extinct."

"She's lost a lot of blood."

"We're going to take her into the operating room. You said she's been shot?"

"It was an accident."

"Why don't you bring her in so we can get started."

Max follows Messynda a few steps before he notices Gimmee isn't following. "Aren't you coming?"

"No. Just... Mentally narrate whatever's happening, OK?"

"OK."

Max turns back to Messynda, who's eyeing at him strangely.

"What just happened there?" she asks. "It looked like you two were communicating?"

"Not really." He brushes past her, but then doesn't know which way to go. He waits for her to brush past him again, through the operating room door. Upon entering, as he takes in the rows of cold metal instruments, some gleaming, some dull. His heart sinks.

"You can stay or go," says Messynda. "It's totally up to you. If you can stomach the sight of blood, you can stay."

"I'll stay."

Messynda tears a length of paper from a large roll on the wall dispenser and pulls it over the metal operating table. Gently, she takes Warin from Max's arms and lays her out on it. Warin looks small on the table. Messynda washes her hands, rubs them with a disinfecting gel and puts on a pair of rubber gloves.

"We're ready to start."

She disinfects the wound on Warin's side and applies a red dye to it. She pokes at it with a slim rod.

Max grimaces in anticipatory pain. "Aren't you going to use an anesthetic?"

"I will. I just need to get a sense of what's going on in there first."

"But she might wake up."

With a scalpel, Messynda makes an incision to expand the wound opening. A whine cuts through Max's mind, so powerful that he falls to his knees, clutching his head.

Messynda stares at him. "What was that?"

"Nothing. I got a sudden headache." He climbs back to his feet.

"No, I felt it too. As if I'd heard something, only not through my ears."

"Maybe you're developing a headache. I've changed my mind, I can't stay here to watch the operation. I'm going back to the waiting room."

Messynda nods. "Of course. And you were right, I should apply anesthetic right away."

As Max reaches the door, Messynda calls out, "She's

quite special, isn't she? I mean, she's special in a way that most people wouldn't believe."

Max nods. He pushes through the door to the waiting room.

"Where are you going?" says Gimmee as Max walks past him. "You're supposed to be my eyes and ears in there."

"I can't do it. We're going to have to just wait and see."

"Thanks for consulting me on this, Max. I'm so lucky to have you."

"I'm going outside to make a phone call."

Night has fallen. The outside sky is full of stars. In the silence, every step Max makes crunches in the gravel of the path that leads to the parking lot.

He calls Tascha.

"I'm at the veterinarian's. Warin is being seen to."

"Is she OK?"

"The veterinarian is operating on her right now."

"Will she be OK?"

"I don't know yet."

"Why didn't you wait until after to call me?"

"Tascha, I was thinking. How about you keep the house and I keep the store?"

"You want the store? You can have it. I'm going to sell the house and move somewhere."

"That's good. Make a new start."

"I have to. Sometimes you just have to wipe everything out to make a new start. The Institute program was exactly what we needed at the time, but we're different people now."

"I'm not convinced we really needed it. All the memories I now have from before the Institute program come from a comic book. The worst part of it is, my comic book memories feel real, as real as anything I've known since."

"Well, my memories are real." Tascha falls silent a long moment. "Yeah, I need to start over again."

"I'll let you know how the operation goes."

Max hangs up. He walks back to the hospital entrance. Gimmee is peering at him through the wall-high waiting room window. He's standing on the top of a chair, his long tail swishing around nervously.

"Max, Get me out of here! It's too loud, Max!"

Gimmee taps frenetically against the glass with the claws of both hands.

Max opens the entrance door open to let him out.

25

Eva enters the bar on bring-your-own-culture night, glides to her regular seat, removes her raincoat. She folds it neatly in four and places it in a corner to prevent anyone sitting on it. She sits and begins mouthing the words to the song she's prepared for the evening, humming to herself in a low voice. The regular crowd hasn't arrived yet, the bar is mostly empty. She gazes around, warmed by its familiarity. This is home.

Fimandi pushes off the bar, his momentum carrying him off toward Eva's table.

"Eva."

Eva looks up, mouths a few more words to her song, pauses.

"Hi, Fimandi." Her voice is chipper, politely welcoming.

"You're here early." He looks around. "There's no one here yet. It might be a slow night."

Eva shrugs. "Oh well."

"Can I buy you a beer?" asks Fimandi.

"Thanks, I'm alright."

"I'll buy you a beer."

"I'm alright."

"Eva."

"Yes?"

Fimandi sits down next to her. She smiles politely. He smiles too, placating, puckering the corner of his lips.

"Eva, I know we've drifted apart. I'm not blind."

"Oh, I don't know."

"I know we've drifted apart and I want you to know that it doesn't lessen my affection for you."

Eva looks down.

"So let me buy you a fucking beer."

She laughs. "OK Fimandi. Buy me a fucking beer. And I'll fucking drink it."

He nods, leans forward and kisses her temple. She rests her head against the kiss. He puts an arm around her shoulder, gives her a little squeeze.

"OK," he says.

"OK," she echoes. She nods. He stands and goes back to the bar.

Eva smoothes her hair, takes a deep breath, resumes humming and mouthing the words to her song.

...

Tascha and Frin are heading home in the van. Tascha's driving.

"You're not saying much," she says.

Frin stares out the window, doesn't reply.

"Are you angry?"

"I'm irritated."

"Is it about the store?"

"I can't believe you just gave him the store."

"Well, I don't want it."

"You knew he wanted the store."

"I knew it because he told me so. He called me to tell."

"Your loyalty is still to Max, isn't it?"

"No."

"Really? I think your loyalty is still to Max. After all we've been in together, after all I've done to guide you back into a serene mental space. Max asks for the store and you just give it to him."

"I don't want the store."

"You didn't consult me, Tascha. You didn't ask me what I wanted."

"Do you want the store?"

"No."

"So, let Max have it. He has plans for it."

"My point is, you didn't consult me."

"I was thinking we should sell the house, move away, make a new start."

Frin doesn't answer immediately. "We'd have to go

somewhere where there's an Extrapolist church we can join."

"That certainly narrows down the possibilities."

"That's the condition." Frin turns to stare out the window.

"It actually makes it easier to decide where to go," remarks Tascha. "There aren't too many places with an Extrapolist church."

She yawns. "It'll be your turn to drive soon. I need a nap."

The van hums along, reverberating to the road's texture. Tascha rolls down a window, letting the cool air in. She thrusts an arm out, tasting the oncoming wind on her bare skin. It tickles. She splays out her fingers, lets her arm sway back and forth.

"Actually, I don't need a nap. I'm OK. I can go all night."

Up ahead, the road disappears into darkness.

About the Author

René Ghosh was born in Montréal, Canada in 1972. He has been living in Paris, France since 1999.

The Memory Monkey is his third novel.